A. F. Roberts

ISBN 978-1-0980-2125-2 (paperback)
ISBN 978-1-0980-2126-9 (digital)

Christian Faith Publishing, Inc.
832 Park Avenue
Meadville, PA 16335
www.christianfaithpublishing.com

Printed in the United States of America

And as they did eat, Jesus took bread and blessed and brake it, and gave to them and said, "Take, eat; this is my body."

And he took the cup and when he had given thanks, he gave it to them: and they all drank of it. And he said unto them, "This is my blood of the new testament, which is shed for many. Verily I say unto you, I will drink no more of the fruit of the vine, until that day that I drink it new in the kingdom of God."

—Mark 14: 22–25

PROLOGUE

The Caribbean, 1790

The island looked peaceful and beautiful enough when we approached it; why wouldn't it when you've sailed the Caribbean and come to an isle such as St. Vincent? But when you're on a missionary journey to reach out to a native tribe in hopes of conversion, you never *truly* know what you're getting into, no matter how idyllic it looks at the beginning nor how sure you are of your faith.

As far as we knew, we were simply representing the Holy Catholic Church of England to share Christ Jesus with the indigenous peoples. We trekked from the shores on inland, searching for signs of habitation. We found it slowly, frightfully, when jungle sounds came to us from this way and that. Animals? Tribesmen? We couldn't know until they were upon us, surrounding us, taking us. We spoke out, cried out to them, of Jesus's love and peace to all men. Oh, if only the Holy Ghost had come and opened their ears to our tongue and ours to theirs. But He did not come, not this day.

Some of us, though not antagonistic, *did* attempt some defense against our impending capture. Those who did paid the price in being beaten and were unconscious by the time we reached their village. Those, such as myself who did not, were simply led away by force by these clansmen.

They were ghastly, faces painted with a white chalky substance encircling their eyes and mouths. It was like blackface, eerie and disturbing. Their camp was equally frightening. I saw a pot with a duck's flesh, goose flesh and a man's. There was likewise the head of a young man fastened to a post, still *bleeding,* and drinking vessels made of skulls. I noted also the bones of men's arms and legs on the heads of their arrows. The reports of Columbus's travels in this area were starting to dawn on me as to just what kind of natives it appeared we'd been sent to reach, natives with whom you do not survive the encounter.

I *did,* but only I alone. And only after being prodded and poked to reveal that I was undefiled by man. As such, I was a delicacy—one I would be preserved for to *drink,* not eat. Not as the rest of my companions were.

Over time, my spirit was beaten and broken, my blood drained and drunk. I said I'd lived but only after a fashion. I was undead in *their* sins.

CHAPTER 1

Charissa

I awoke this day as I do most days—late in the afternoon, a little prior to dusk. It is not because I am anchored into an employ such as a graveyard shift; I am self-employed, and the "work" I do is best served in the night. A night owl I suppose you could call me, but that is more due to the state of my existence, rather than any preferential bent to the time of day in which I thrive.

My occupation might be called morally suspect, but it serves well to meet my needs for survival. I escort gentlemen in this city of Chicago, where I have found myself living for the better portion of a century. I offer companionship, coupled with a mixture of pleasure and pain. And in that *pain*, I find the blurred line through which I'm able to maintain my true sustenance without great risk of detection or commission of murder. *Far* more civilized than the way in which I was born into this cannibalistic life. I neither relish nor disdain what it is I do nor what my being entails. It simply *is*, and like most, I carry on with what I must.

On occasion such as today, I'll note the calendar, noticing some religious observance, which takes me back to a time long ago, when I sought to meet men's spiritual rather than carnal needs. My mental note saw that this was Good Friday, which stopped me, if only for a moment. Quickly, I moved on to preparing for my daily run along Lakeshore Drive. After which I would return to prepare myself for an appointment later in the night.

I moved out from my flat, stretching, limbering myself up, ready to set my pace. Before I knew it, I was once more gliding upon my path, taking in the view of the bay, and running strong. And I *am* strong. A strong woman, a strong entity. I've outlived countless generations of those who are the age I *appear* to be. It is truly mesmerizing to me that the young woman's visage, which shows upon my face would actually be that of an old sage, if I aged as normal humans do. But no matter, I am what I am, and I accept it, even embrace it at times. Other times, not so much. And this would be one of those days as soon as I turned a corner and headed inland into Old Town.

Why I deviated from my regular course, who knew, I just did. Maybe it was some subconscious plant from that glance at the calendar, I don't know. What I would learn was that it would be pivotal. As I jogged toward the quaint, little city park, I began to see them. And *him*. The priest leading his little flock to the little park, taking their little mass in a procession of lit little candles across the street to finish it all in the sacrament of Communion; the mortal reflection of what I do literally to survive. Why I didn't keep running ahead or turn around, I wish I knew. I had come to scoff at that particular ceremony, as to me, it was the difference between drinking a putrid light beer as opposed to a strong whiskey.

But slow to a complete stop I did. I still don't know if it was the sheep or their shepherd that captivated me, probably the latter. I huddled next to a tree large enough to block my spying. Or so I thought. Not right away but soon *he* spotted me, met my returned gaze, and did it—*invited* me to join. The fool. And so, too, was I.

Father Christopher

It was dusk on a Good Friday in Old Town, Chicago. My late Mass at St. Michaels Church was winding down with an unconventional procession of the congregation to the outside of the cathedral for Communion.

I am Father Christopher, and I prefer to do things differently. I can't wait for the first chance to get my flock outdoors as winter subsides, a season I disdain. My intent was to get myself and my people out from under their cold weather bundles and back out into the day and the light, even though this *was* dusk technically.

They marched, some of them grumbling under their still slightly frosty breaths, across the street to the grassy backlot of the Parish Center. I had them make their way with candles we lit while still inside to symbolize taking the light of our worship into the outside world.

The point did not go unnoticed, as passersby stopped to look for a moment or two, just to see what was it all about. This particular woman, a lithe jogger, slowed her pace from her route, simply to satisfy her curiosity.

As the assembly settled into our destination, they extinguished the candles so that they next could take Communion. The ushers appeared with wine and bread and prepared to serve as soon as I finished my recital of the elements. I gave thanks both unto God, as well as my parishioners for coming along to participate in the slightly unorthodox activity.

The woman named Charissa, as I would later learn, had come to a full halt at this juncture, her attention garnered at our peculiar behavior. Perhaps it struck her that it was a tad too early in the season for such a thing? But then again, she was out *jogging*, after all. The unusual spin our group had taken in the activity apparently left her unable to dismiss it and continue her run. She, too, settled in, huddled up to a tree, blowing upon her hands for warmth, as she continued to observe us.

I could never have known that what I did next would change everything for me, and for her, from then on. Having seen her *see* us, I paused to strike out to *invite* her to join. Initially, she rejected the invitation, but I, fool that I am, continued to press.

"I don't care much for religious ceremony any longer," Charissa said. "I'm one of God's abandoned projects," she concluded.

Not accepting of such a mind-set, I coaxed, replying, "God has no projects He abandons, my dear. Perhaps 'construction' has merely been delayed. Please join in. Share a moment with us, as we close, then return to your run."

She reluctantly acquiesced, stepping out from behind the tree, and came into our midst. I returned to my post, redirecting to the passing out of the elements, and our Communion, with our new guest, and commenced.

"The body of Christ," I said, "take, eat." After which, I recited, "The blood of Christ, drink." As the passing cup finally came upon Charissa, I noted a distinct hesitation on her part to continue. Upon which, I met her eyes with mine and nodded as though in blessing to do so.

She sighed, closed her eyes, took the cup to her lips, and swallowed some wine. When she opened them again and handed the cup back off, they were dilated, almost as though fueled somehow. I know it must have been my imagination, but they seemed to appear as if red. It was clear that she became aware that I noticed, as she quickly turned away from my gaze. I equally shifted my attention elsewhere as I immediately felt disturbed.

I proceeded from that point to focus only upon concluding the Mass, greeting and dismissing my congregation, with only an occasional glance back to her direction. And every time I did, she seemed to be locked in place, brooding, interacting with no one, only an incidental strained smile to keep them moving past and away from her.

And despite her now apparent disinterest in remaining, she *did*. Remain, that is, as if waiting for everyone else to depart, waiting for me.

CHAPTER 2

Charissa

I knew better. I should have just kept running by them all. Not glanced, not blinked, and especially not stopped. Yet there I was. Afire. My thirst burning for blood. His blood. Stupid priest, noticing me, inviting me to join in. And me, *stupid* for allowing myself to be sucked into it all.

I stood there, letting the cup come to me and took it. I even stopped, ready to pass it along to the next person. Then *his* eyes met mine again. He nodded, and I went right on ahead and did it. Curse me! And then I waited and burned. I didn't want to even be there, yet I smiled and nodded people past me. And he talked with them, said hello and goodbye, and it was all so wonderful. But we both knew that it would come down to he and I remaining alone. And I couldn't wait. I should've left with the rest, but I could not. I had to finish what *he* had started.

Finally, there we were, only he and I, by ourselves in that park. I approached. "So, Priest, are you happy still, that I joined you? Prompted me beyond my better judgment to participate? You must sense by now that this was not wise, yes?"

"Yeess," he slowly, hesitantly replied. He didn't know *why*, but he knew.

"Come, Man of God, walk with me, as I must now also prompt *you*," I said. We walked back across the street toward his parish.

"Call me Christopher," was his only answer then. "Father Christopher. And though I find myself growing somewhat uneasy with you, I'm still pleased to meet you, Miss—?"

"I am Charissa," I said, pausing, then laughing, though slightly madly.

"And what might you find so suddenly humorous, my dear?" he questioned, trying to mask his ever-growing uneasiness with me.

"Our names, sir," I answered. "We're *both* Chris for short. Is that not just too ironic?"

"I suppose that it *could* be, Charissa, but I do not see—"

"You have *supposed* too much and *see* too little, my new friend. Now, please, take my humorous observance and heed it. My full name, just as yours, is far too formal, as we are about to become more intimate," I said, taking his hand and looking into his eyes. "Call me Chris, and I shall call you the same." As I held his one hand in both of mine, we were on the steps of the church's entrance, and I continued to hold my stare upon him. I raised the hand to my face and rubbed the wrist upon my cheek. Still keeping my gaze to his, I turned my neck so that the wrist next passed my lips and then I bit. And I *took*, and I *drank*.

Father Christopher

I stood there upon the church steps after the Mass's commencement at the parish's park. I watched the mysterious woman I'd invited for communion trot off and away. Somehow, the time from when we'd finished at the park to when I got back seemed vague, missing.

I remembered everyone else had gone, and she and I remained. I think we'd talked and walked a bit, but then, I'm not sure. Finally, I watched her disappear completely out of sight and felt bewildered.

I scratched an itch upon my wrist, opened the door, and returned inside. My ushers, who had come back before me, had taken care of our leftover bread, cups, and bloo—er, wine. Why did *blood* come to mind first? I wondered. No doubt the parallel in symbolism to Christ's essence poured out for us. I scratched at my wrist again.

I caught a glance from Paul, one of the ushers, that read peculiar toward me, that is to say. In as much as I was feeling that way already, I simply came clean to him right then. "I know that was very odd, even for me, inviting an utter stranger to come and join us like that. It's just, the way she was lingering about, I felt prompted to do so."

He replied, "Well, it *did* seem unorthodox that you not even ask if she was Catholic, sir. But I do see your point in taking the communion outdoors to blend it into the community. The weird part was *her* afterward, hanging around till everyone was gone to apparently get you alone. I wasn't sure I should leave you to go ahead and bring things back, but you nodded that it was okay."

I did? I thought, having no recollection of having done so or the entire walk back with her from the park for that matter. Still, I answered, fudging, "Yes, I did, and it was fine. I thought perhaps I'd known her from someplace and wished to pursue it to see if I was right."

"And?" asked Paul.

My answer that came out surprised me, as it only occurred in that very instant. "She was no one I've ever interacted with before, but I think I may have passed her once or twice, out jogging." And though at that point, any more of my responses to his queries were only to defer the conversation to a halt, I was finding that the reply *was* accurate.

Perhaps it was my lack of remembrance in the time gap between park and here that pushed this notion forth, but it rang true. I believed, in that moment, that I had *indeed* crossed paths with Charissa during a run, if only in passing. Suddenly, a feeling of wanting to do so—run—flushed over me. And peculiar upon peculiar, it wasn't just my own desire to want to run; it was some kind of shared adrenalin rush with *hers*—the one I knew she must still now be in, as it was only minutes ago I'd seen her dash off. I felt as if my own blood was pumping like unto a run's exertion even though I was standing still.

CHAPTER 3

Charissa

I was still running, though at that moment, I almost felt like I'd stopped. But I surely didn't want to. Stop, that is. I wanted to run as far and as fast as I could from whence I'd come. To have allowed what had just happened—*any* of it—had been sheer foolishness. From the curiosity, to the lingering there, to ultimately, my predator-to-prey behavior at Christopher, and then, in essence, making the kill.

Christopher*? What?* I'd gone from calling him simply Priest to completely eliminating *Father* from before his name in the span of a quarter of an hour? *What has this man done to me?* Or what was it that I'd done to him? To both of us? I could blame him all I wanted, and I *do*, for his shared portion of this mess now created; but in the end, the responsibility lay mostly with me.

As the "older one," by centuries mind you, I should've known far better. But despite all that, it appeared as though I was still capable of being a silly woman, swept away by a man. And an unattainable one, for Christ's sake—literally! For it was unto *Him* that a man I'd momentarily swooned over was given. God Almighty, talk about wanting what you can't have. Except for the fact that I've circumvented that.

Not only did I drink of Christopher, but also I'd comingled *my* blood upon his wrist for healing so that my deception of what I'd done through my stare would be complete. He'd *know* nothing, not even from the now nonexistent wound. But he would start to *feel* things of me. Just as I, now, was starting to feel things of him. Why else would I have the sensation of having stopped, though still running? Because *he* was at rest, I presumed. And he, more than likely, would now be feeling like he was running because *I was! Good going,* Charissa, *good going.*

At last I shook myself out of my self-abuse, remembering I had things to attend to after what was supposed to be an uneventful run. I had a client to escort and *punish* before too long. Somehow though, *that* part—the part that's the core reason for doing it all in the first place—wasn't holding its usual interest for me. And not just because I'd already had a little "snack." I think it was who—and what—I'd snacked *on*: a man who's lifeblood flows in things of the eternal. Do my typical cliental dwell upon such? No, they think only of the moment, of the fleeting excitement I provide to them in scant pockets of time. That is why it is only a job to me and a meal.

Ahh, but Christopher! He could appreciate the steadfastness of longsuffering for things that will last, just as *I've* lasted for so long. Not eternally, of course, but at times I felt like I *have* lived forever. Sort of unto those people of the Old Testament who were recorded to have lived anywhere from five to nine hundred years. Now, there were some folks I can relate to. Yes, I know my Bible to a good degree. After all, it was the word of God I once lived to proclaim before this life of blood sustenance happened to me. And it *was* the mission field that led me to this wretched fate.

Surprising that I should call it such when I say that I accept what I am? It is true that I do, but I also say "some days, not so much." And this was turning out to be the ultimate one of those days to the extent that I'd actually called it "a cursed thing." Again, my foolish comingling with Christopher. Was he now becoming my priest, my *escort* as it were, to the God who'd left me behind? Or had I left Him? Time would most certainly tell; and I know a little something about the passing of time.

Father Christopher

I'd wanted to go and run then, but I didn't. Night had nearly fallen by that time, and I was not one to go for a run in Chicago after dark. I felt about the same toward the night as I do about winter. Besides, it was just not wise. Still, I was very keyed up, and yes, clearly over Charissa. So instead I thought it *was* wise to work on a liturgy for Easter morning, only little more than a day away.

Yet as I'd soon find, there would be none of the material I could work on that wouldn't make me think of blood. *His* blood. And *her* blood? Why Charissa's blood? What could possibly be the significance of that? I pondered for some moments, and my mind poured back to something I *could* remember from the Lord's supper, with her in the park. That being, when the cup came to her and she hesitated. Almost as though she had some superstition or aversion to it. It was only when I nodded to her that it was all right did she drink; and after *that*, something seemed like it came over her, something not right.

Perhaps she had an ultrasensitive spirit to the transubstantiation process so that when I'd blessed it and the wine *became* Christ's blood, the consumption thereof was too much for her? I couldn't say, and my mind couldn't get any further around it just then, but more certainly would come later when I slept and dreamt.

Before long, as the outline for the liturgy began to come together, I checked out—of consciousness, that is. As often happens to people while reading or writing, my vision strayed. I became weary, and my head bobbed up and down, trying to fight the nap that was coming on. A fight I finally lost.

Then I became lost in dreaming somewhere between Christ and Charissa. The liturgy conception of his death and resurrection was the first imagery to present itself. He was there upon the cross surrounded by the Marys—His Mother, *her* sister, and Magdalene. As the story goes, after saying "Behold thy Mother/Son," He said, "I thirst." Then the setting rewound to Him with the Samaritan woman at the well, where He continued seamlessly from the former saying, "Give me to drink."

After her pronouncement that He had nothing to draw with, the script took on a life of its own. She drew, turned around, and appeared as Charissa! She offered Him a drink of her own waterpot, and He did. He returned it to her, and she refreshed herself as well. When she pulled it away from her mouth, however, it wasn't water that trickled off her lips but blood, and her eyes went red. This image at last stunned me awake, shuddering.

As the initial shock began to fade, I began trying to process the meaning of it all. First, her eyes being red brought back another snippet of lost recollection from Communion in the park. I remembered her eyes not red but dilated after finally drinking the wine, which confirmed to me my previous suspicion that she was not only sensitive to the sacrament but also perhaps had a deeper understanding of it than I ever could have guessed. But what could *that* understanding specifically be, I wondered.

I thought further about the John 4 account of *living water* Jesus talked to the woman about, and she wanted it. Then I thought about John 19 where he spoke of the soldier's spear piercing the Lord's side, and out coming water and blood. So likely therein lay the connection. The *water* that gives *life* is the blood, and Charissa somehow comprehends this better perhaps than most.

Although the entire assessment made perfect sense to me, I felt like I was missing something, that there was still a bigger picture to it all that I had yet to grasp. But what else could there be?

I shook my head, also shaking off the Charissa mystery for now. My Easter preparations weren't going to get done by themselves. So I continued on with that for a time, at last calling it a night some hours later. I retired, then dreamt more again of He and her.

CHAPTER 4

Charissa

Johnathon O'Connor was one of my more sophisticated clients. When we met for a night's session, it was in a more professional manner—that being dinner at a nice restaurant first, *then* our dessert of "playtime," so to speak. John was a well-groomed bearded man and an advertising executive. He was tall with a medium build—just what I like to work with.

He certainly would have joined me in a drink, but he was a recovering alcoholic, so he had water with lemon while I nursed my sangria. He had just finished an amusing joke, then took a drink of water. Right after that, I'd taken another sip of wine, still giggling a little from the punch line. In so doing, a small trickle of wine escaped the corner of my mouth.

And at that instant, God only knows why, I felt like our moment had been observed—by Christopher? My attention then darted around the room, looking for him. Of course, he was not here; why would he be? I was being silly, letting my imagination get the best of me. But why *that*, of all things? Unless this damn connection I'd created with our comingling of blood was somehow finding deeper cracks in our consciousnesses. And if that *was* the case, would he begin to see what would ensue as mine and John's evening progressed? That would be all I'd need—a priest seeing what I do literally for a living.

John quickly saw that I was distracted and queried if anything was wrong. I replied that there wasn't, just some rubbish that I had a lot on my mind lately. He and I both agreed that it wouldn't be long until our extracurricular activity would certainly take care of that!

And upon returning to the basement dungeon of my flat, we commenced to do just that. In the old days, when I'd first begun this little circus show, I would blindfold my clients so they wouldn't see me when I'd climaxed the activities, biting and drinking from them. That had gone wrong a time or two, with a neck getting gouged out when they didn't like things going to that extreme. I'd since learned to abandon the blindfold and let my hypnotic prowess take care of things. After all, the entire scenario was all predicated by *my* control and being the dominant. So it was basically a perfect segue. All of this to keep me from being a killer, only taking what I need *without* utterly ending lives, sometimes making more undead ones.

As the session wore on, I started experiencing a decidedly unwanted phenomenon. I began visualizing Christ being whipped prior to his execution. And naturally, being what I am, the blood-letting that comes with a scourging roused my thirst even more. Christ—Christ-opher. Dammit, that priest was somehow doing it to me again!

Fortunately, with my little Christopher snack from earlier, I was able to fight off my blood urges until the session had reached its height, and I only drew from John when it was actually time. Had I given in and drank of him early, he likely would've been suspicious as to why our time had reached its conclusion so soon. And John's a man who likes to get *all* he's paid for. And so it went; our evening finished and compensated. He gave me a friendly kiss goodbye as I escorted him out into the night.

I returned back up to the living space of the flat and began pondering more the strangeness of what happened during the session. It wasn't that I *never* thought of God or his Son at all but certainly not to the extent that I once did. And *certainly* not while I was working. There were rules in the workplace at large not to mix religion and the job. And this was why it *was* a distraction. Or perhaps it was that I'd feel ashamed of what God would think of what I do? I could, of course, rationalize to Him the righteousness of it all in the avoidance of "Thou shalt not kill" but truly, could, *would,* God really buy that? I rather doubt it.

After I'd wrestled with this for a time, I decided to dash the thought, have some more wine, and read a book. It helped, but the lingering thought that these connections were growing in their frequency, I still found it troublesome. If it persisted, I would almost certainly have to deal with it and seek out its source once more—Christopher.

Father Christopher

I'd woken again in the wee morning hours, after more unsettling dreams. At first there was a man, bearded, much as I suppose we imagine the Lord to look like, although certainly *not* Jewish. He'd been captured—no, only *appeared* that way. I think he was that way of his own volition, welcoming the punishment he was receiving from Charissa, naturally. I began to wonder what kind of predator this woman actually was, considering the visions I was having of her.

Then the scene changed, and it truly *was* Jesus being whipped, not that I actually *saw* her on the other end of the cat o' nine tails. Nonetheless, I *felt* her arousal, not sexually, thank God but at the blood. *The blood*—stimulating? How insane was that? Who *was* she? And then I found out. The scene changed back to the original man, and she was biting him in the neck. Like a…a…vampire. After which, the scene changed yet again, bringing back my own, apparently forgotten memory. She was still biting, but this time, it was upon *my* wrist, there, on the steps outside the church where we'd been when while walking and talking. And that, of course, was what woke me up, shuddering once again.

It was at that point I'd had enough of it all. I looked at the clock: it was 4:00 a.m. Still dark but dawn would not be that far off. I decided then and there to at last go for that run I'd put off late yesterday. To hell with the early morning cold that would greet me when I stepped outside; some extra layers would take care of that, because right now, I *needed* a run.

CHAPTER 5

Charissa

I hadn't gone running then *with* the specific intent of looking for the priest; I simply wanted *out* from my place, from my thoughts. After the reading and the wine hadn't entirely done their job, I couldn't think of a better purge than the adrenaline rush of a run. The idea had struck me around 3:00 a.m. I was ready and out the door by 3:30.

I knew dawn was not too far off, but I'd not planned to go far—Schiller Street to Lakeshore Drive, and on to Concrete Beach. I like my runs to be along Lake Michigan as much as possible. Being originally from London, I loved the Thames and the North Sea. So here in America, my loves had become the Great Lakes. Apparently, I was not the only one who felt that way.

As I headed south from Schiller along Lakefront Trail, I sensed him. I'd say "spotted" him, but that would be impossible, as he was to my rear. That would be *his* job, to identify me. Even if I'd not been in the lead, one wouldn't likely recognize a priest not in his normal attire anyway. I, on the other hand, would be far more distinguishable to him, as this was just how I looked when he'd first met me.

I didn't want to turn around at all, tipping him off that I might know he was there. I thought I felt his pace slow a little, perhaps in hesitation from pinpointing me. After all, if my experiences of late were any indication, who knows *what* he'd been seeing of me. And if he'd seen enough, he could be afraid to get too close. So I decided to play with him a little and see how interested he was at the prospect of another encounter. God knew we *really* should talk.

I picked up my pace and started to sprint. I smiled as I heard his footfalls increase. Good, he would give chase. This was nice; the sources of each of our frustrations, *each other,* were being worked out in physical exertion together. What could possibly be more perfect or ironic? *My* being caught in the sunrise perhaps? As they say in this day and age, that would suck. I stopped suddenly and immediately. He wasn't ready for that. I turned around to face him.

I thought at first to be formal, but then when I spoke, I simply said, "Hello, Chris."

He replied, "Chris," with a nod, which was what I was hoping for in addressing him in the short. *If* he acquiesced, the building tensions of this meeting might be reduced. He hunched over, leaning his hands down upon his knees, breathing hard. As he remained crouched, he lifted one arm and wiggled his wrist.

"Tell me about this," he said.

I walked straight up to him, took the hand, and helped him up. This was a good, friendly start. Then I took the risk of ruining it, but I had to confirm what I presumed he meant.

"Do you mean this?" I asked, pulling the wrist slowly toward my mouth and clacking my teeth. I moved my fingers from the wrist into his palm, returning his hand to him. I squeezed it briefly as I let it go, again to indicate care, not hostility in any way.

"Yes," he said, *"that.* What did you do? What I *saw* while dreaming?"

"Ah," I replied. "You are connecting to me in dreams. I am to you while I'm awake. In either case, it *is* my fault. What I've *done* has bonded us through our blood and the comingling of it. A thousand apologies. It should never have happened. Though *you* do shoulder some blame in your persistence for me to join your ceremony, I'll have you know. You must know also that I've not a lot of time left this morn, out of doors anyway. The daylight is not good for me. Might we run together and return now? I can elaborate more on the way"

He nodded, and as he did I gently breezed his arm with my hand, turning to lead the way. Again, I did so in a friendly manner. He flinched slightly, but was not off-putting. Though his presence in my life now was a growing annoyance, I still found that, while I was actually *with* him, I think I actually liked him.

Father Christopher

So there we were, this femme fatale and the priestly padre, running together from Concrete Beach along Lakefront Trail. I hadn't been looking for her in these predawn hours; I just needed clear her from my thoughts. It was said in church culture that *intention is everything.* If this was so, it *was* happening, though in a curiously counteractive way.

I'm not much for talking while I run, so I simply listened to her as she talked and ran, neither seeming to interfere with her breathing while she did. If she indeed *was* what had been deduced in my dreams, this would make perfect sense.

She only offered up a brief introduction to it all, as our jog time was short. She explained quite simply that she was once a child of the light and now was a creature of the night.

"My prior life," she'd begun, "*was* serving the Lord of grace and light. I'd served to the extent of traveling into the mission fields—native and uncivilized tribes of the deepest of jungles. What we didn't know going in was that those we visited were actually cannibals. Sadly, we would find out the hard way. I was ultimately the only survivor of my group, if you can call what became of me surviving."

"I'm sorry," I said, briefly offering all I would say while we still ran.

Before long, we slowed to a cool-down pace toward her residence when she replied, "I'm sorry, too, I haven't told you very much, really. And I do have to go inside now."

"Might I come in then?" I asked. "I don't share your aversion to the sun, but I *do* hate the cold."

She laughed heartily and commented to the irony, "*You* asking *me* to come in! That's funny, it should be the other way around, wouldn't you agree?"

"I suppose so," I said smiling, though not nearly as amused as she.

"I'm not sure coming in right now is the best idea just yet, Father," she replied. "This blood bond I've created between us doesn't need any extra help in our getting too familiar with each other, I'd say. Again, my apologies to that, *I'm* sorrier than you know. Although it wouldn't do *me* much good, I could offer you another little dose of hypnosis. You know, to try and help dissuade the connection, the dreams."

"I'll be fine," I said, not quite being truthful. I actually didn't know if I would be or not, but I wasn't sure I wanted to go down that road again, deleting memory. Then *I* had an idea. "Perhaps, if you'd like to speak more, and I would much like to *hear* more, you could come to the church and join me in, say, the confessional. It *is* very private."

She laughed aloud again, this time actually cocking her head backward and holding her chest. Not the reaction I was truly after; a simple yes or no would have sufficed.

Once she regained her composure, she said, "I'm sorry, I didn't mean to laugh so hard. I was just imagining espousing my horrid history to you in confession. I don't know, I'm still trying to get past the satire of it. Perhaps, we'll see."

"Or maybe we can just run again," I said, backpedaling to a simpler Plan B.

"Perfect," she said, "I'd like that, and I'll think about coming to the church. It's not far after all. In the meantime, let's *test* our connection. I don't want your number nor do I want to give you mine. If it continues the way it's been so far, I'm guessing we'll be able to rendezvous *without* actually calling one another. Are you game?"

"Perhaps, we'll see," I said, quoting her, and this time, *I* laughed.

She giggled along with, then grabbed my hands and said, "I *have* to go. The sun's coming up, goodbye."

"Wait, one more second please," I said. "You never really said *why* you bit me in the first place, Charissa—"

"All I can say is that it was impulse, an urge I couldn't suppress once you'd prompted me to take the sacrament. So, your fault, my fault, it doesn't matter anymore; it's done. And now I really *must* go. I'll see you soon, Christopher."

With that, she shut the door and closed the conversation. Having no further business here, I turned back up Hudson Street to return to the church.

CHAPTER 6

Charissa

I went up the stairs to my apartment and watched him sprint away when I got to an inside window. I suspected he neither cared to linger longer in the neighborhood nor remain in the cold; he'd said as much. Perhaps I should have let him in? No, I stood fast to my decision; he didn't need to be anywhere near my playroom, not while this bond of ours was giving us these insights into each other.

Come to think of it, it *was* rather forward for him, as a priest, to wish to enter a lady's abode, especially with him receiving these specific perceptions of me. You'd think he'd want to do just the opposite—turn tail and run fast and far. Then again, maybe he was feeling sorry for me, considering what I'd shared of my fate on the mission field. Or perhaps, he was growing fond of my company, as I was of his.

No matter. There were greater concerns to ponder as I was reminded upon glancing at the calendar again. Only a day away loomed—Easter Sunday. Though *I* no longer paid a great deal of heed to it, *he'd* be performing multiple masses on that day, numerous services that would include more servings of the Lord's Supper. Knowing what had already transpired between us with but *one* communion and its aftershocks, I shuddered to think what havoc many portions of the meal might wreck on me, on us.

All the speaking he'd be doing of Christ's sacrifice of *lifeblood,* all the *blood wine* that would be consumed, there was no way of knowing what kind of psychic overdose it might produce. As my occupation entails, I am an expert in the realm of control; but in facing *this,* I feared my threshold could be pushed beyond its limit. And what his tolerances were, I had no idea. Perhaps it was indeed time to give serious thought to going to him in the confessional.

So much for my grand idea of *not* exchanging numbers; I probably would've called him right away to set something up. As it was, I would simply have to try and reach him dreaming, as I went into my daytime rest. Clergymen lived a different lifestyle than that of the average working man, I surmised. Maybe he'd be more apt to adhere to a naptime during the course of the day? I'd have to go with that possibility and keep busy cleaning up my place for the duration of the morning, then settle into sleep as the afternoon drew nigh.

Father Christopher

By the time I'd arrived back at the parish, the sun was shining, and I was very glad to be home. Though Charissa's apartments were nice, they bordered some unsavory streets; and some of the residents there might be considered suspect themselves. Of course, *she* was as well, so I'm sure she got along just fine. I've worked in the area myself for neighborhood outreach; but still, for as early as we'd been running, trouble could've been lurking around any corner. It was good to be out of the cold as well.

I imagine that I avoided some very probable trouble anyway by her refusal to my coming inside with her. It was certainly out of character for me to ask in the first place, but I really *had* wanted to hear more. And I believe this odd connection we'd begun to establish played its part also. I found myself wondering if it would subside or increase as more time went by. Hopefully the former, with Easter Sunday on the horizon. If this blood bond should amplify rather than diminish, it struck me that the holiday observance could hold all manner of mental backlash for us both. *Not* a particularly comforting thought.

I set out then to the more routine and mundane concerns of the day—a meeting with the bishops, schedules, activities, and of course, tomorrow's masses. By the early afternoon, I was ready for a nap, having begun this day at a truly Godforsaken hour. So for the space of slightly under an hour, I caught up on some much needed rest. And I dreamt this time, solely of *her*.

As I would find out upon the hour's conclusion, it would prove to be more than a mere dream but a communication. When it began, I was in the cathedral alone, attending to the altar, placing candles and wine goblets where they should go for Mass.

I was interrupted by the arrival of Charissa through the front door. She stalked in confidently, striding down the aisle, looking right at me, then turning left at the break in the rear to front pews. She nodded to me as she did, darting directly toward the confessionals. She went inside; I followed.

When I entered and pulled the screen open, I said, "Hello, Chris," as I felt we were getting further and further from formalities as we went.

"Chris," she returned. "I'm no expert by any means in dreaming to another, but when you said how much you picked up on while *you were*, it seemed only natural to try and reach you in this way. Luckily, it appears you're napping, and I, of course, slumber during the day. I have concerns about tomorrow. I don't say this often, and we *are* in a confessional after all. I confess that I'm afraid."

"I share your concern," I began. "It has occurred to me also that if this bond does not lessen, we could be in for all manner of visions, or worse. I don't know, do you?"

"I do not," she said. "I've turned only a handful of souls in this lengthy life of mine, and though through *that* an intriguing bond is formed, I've never experienced anything quite like this. If you were to say in some priestly-like manner that God himself is trying to do a work in this, I might just be inclined to believe it."

"I wasn't," I replied, "but it is an excellent point. I wouldn't disagree with you in the least."

"Perhaps I'll have a future as a nun by the end of all this then," she said sarcastically.

"A bit of a stretch, from vampire to nun, don't you think, my dear?" I answered in mutually dry humor.

"Touché," she said. "Moving on, I'd decided, obviously, to take you up on the idea of chatting here. I've spoken now in this dream space *of it*, what I'd intended to come and say to you in person. And I still might later, when the sun sets, if you'll have me. We could discuss this further, as well as tell you of the horrors of my past, my rebirth, if you're still interested."

"Of course," I naturally replied. "And an after-dark meeting should be fine. It will be perfectly private for us. You recall your way here, yes?"

"Of course," she answered. "I couldn't forget how to get there if I tried."

"You know, that brings up a good question," I began, wondering about this. "You like to run by the lake, do you not? From where you live and where the lake is, it doesn't make sense that you would've passed by the church to have caught the communion. How did that happen?"

"You're absolutely right, Chris. Going by the church is entirely not the way I would normally run. As it happened, I was on my *return* from the lake and wanted to stop by Really Good Juice for a smoothie. Yes, even vampires have guilty pleasures. Believe me, after *my* runs I earn them. And then, of course, there was my bonus snack of you."

That seemed a little uncalled for, if you asked me. But that's dreams for you. When I awoke, I was completely clear on all details of the dream, nothing vague nor forgotten. I had complete confidence that we had indeed communicated through it and fully expected to see her back here later.

CHAPTER 7

Charissa

I awoke prior to dusk, my inner clock anxious for the meet I'd set with Christopher earlier in my dreamtime. It had worked exceptionally well; we'd conversed and everything! I suppose I shouldn't have been surprised, considering this quirky bond of ours. Upon shaking off the cobwebs of sleep, it occurred to me that I could have just as easily *called* the church and simply spoken to him. Oh well.

Before long I was showered, dressed, ready, and out the door. It was nice for a change not to be all dolled up in latex, gloves, and boots for an appointment. Although, who knows? Maybe deep down, he'd like that! *Stop it,* Charissa, I told myself. He's a priest, for God's sake!

A few blocks later, I found myself back at the "scene of the crime" upon the steps of St. Michael's where I'd been unable to contain myself only a day ago. And oddly enough, I was back here to see him again. God help me, *this* time I was even going inside! It's been a long time since I've done that: let God help me.

As I went in, it was almost an exact replay of our dream earlier. I strode down the aisle, approaching the break in the pews. He took it upon himself then to alter the script a bit. *As soon* as he saw me, he darted for the confessionals, changing it up so that he would be inside first. I don't know if he thought he was being clever or what. Regardless, I watched which one he went into as I made my left turn at the pew break. I took my time then, letting him *have* his little leg up. I looked around as I walked slowly, letting my mind drift back to when I'd come to these houses, what seemed like a lifetime ago.

At last I entered, adjusting my skirt properly so that I was seated comfortably. Yes, I'd walked my way as a lady, not a jogger. Finally I said, "Forgive me, Father, for I have sinned."

"You have indeed," replied Christopher, blatantly and sarcastically rude for his priestliness.

"I suppose that makes us even for my snide comment of making a snack out of you earlier."

"I think it does," he chuckled in answer. "Seriously now, let's talk about tomorrow and its potential problems for us. We've both had some rather unsettling visions and dreams bouncing back and forth between us. With all the heightened activity of Easter Sunday, I wonder if it could reach a higher threshold, possibly becoming even dangerous for one or both of us. What do you think?"

"I'm concerned as well, Christopher," I began. "Though I'd be sleeping through most of the day, that doesn't mean I'd be immune to the psychic backlash of you and your services. In fact, I'd be quite vulnerable in my unconscious state, I would think."

"Well then? Alternatives? Is it possible for you to get further away in proximity from this neighborhood? Anywhere else you could go? Would that even help?" Chris queried repeatedly.

"I have no idea," I said. "I have a client over in Woodlawn who goes to U of C. I suppose I could contact her. She's about the only one who's relationship has moved beyond client to service provider. I'd call her a friend."

"She?" he stuttered, surprised perhaps that my clientele extended beyond that of men.

"Yes, *she,*" I replied. "I know it's probably unsavory to you, but what I provide *does* stretch farther than the male gender. I apologize, I didn't come here to get into all of *that.* Just so you know, what I do is primarily for my sustenance—without killing. It's questionable, I know, but it provides what I need for food *and* a respectable income."

"I'll simply call it *respectable* that you've found a way to sustain yourself without killing and making more of your kind," he responded.

I surely could have taken prejudicial issue with that last part, but I chose to let it go and not get into an argument. We had bigger concerns just now.

"Thank you," I said matter-of-factly.

"You're welcome," Chris continued. "Do you think that will be far enough away, in Woodlawn?"

"Questionable to be sure. Out of state or further would be preferable, but it's probably the best I can come up with on such short notice. It will have do, I'll call her." I couldn't see him when I said so, but I thought I heard a sigh across our barrier—of relief. Did he, could he, actually *care* about what might happen to me? I've been a lone wolf for so long I'd nearly forgotten what that's like having someone around who gave a damn.

I felt my deadened heart stir. I wanted to put my hand up to the screen between us, that he might take it and share in a brief moment of unison. But I refrained, for fear that I was reaching too far, presuming too much, pushing the envelope farther than it was ready to be opened.

Instead I said simply, "I should go make the call. It's not getting any earlier, and tomorrow *is* only this night away."

"Very well," said Chris. "Normally I wouldn't invite anyone to stay in here for a phone call, but it *is* later, no one else is here, and I probably shouldn't encourage the ladies' room for fear one of the nuns encounter you and wonder about a strange woman being here at this hour."

"Well, we certainly cannot have *that,*" I said sarcastically. At which point, my warming heart froze back to its normal chill once again. "Leave me then, that I may make the call, Father," I said. "I'll meet you by the front door when I'm done and I go."

"Very good," he said. "I'll call for a cab to go to Woodlawn while you're on the phone and accompany you there if you wish."

I smiled and told him thank you very much as he exited, and I began to dial my friend. And my heart began to warm back up once more.

Christopher

Charissa seemed quite at ease, I daresay happy even, on the cab ride to Woodlawn. Yes, her friend and submissive agreed to host her and help out. But I don't think that was what she was smiling shyly about. I think it was because I came with her. And I must say, it pleased me as well somehow.

"Thank you for agreeing to talk in the confessional," I said, trying not to give into the warm, fuzzy feelings I felt surrounding us. "I hope it wasn't too cramped for you."

She laughed. "No, not hardly. If you saw how I sleep, you'd concur."

"Don't tell me it's in a coffin," I replied.

"No but a modern version of one, if you will. I got my hands on a tanning bed from a salon that was closing down. I converted it to my sleeping space, minus all the lighting, of course. More chic for this era, don't you know."

"Interesting. So all the legends are true then? No being in daylight, no entering without invitation, crosses, stakes and the like?"

"To a degree. Obviously, you already know my habits concerning daytime. I'm not going to burn up and turn to ashes if I'm out in it. But I *will* sunburn awfully and get very sick. I've found also that *without* invitation to join someone or enter in, I will get paranoid and obsessive-compulsive to the point of manic-depressive swings. You tend to learn all this over the course of a couple of centuries.

"Speaking of which," she continued on, "as I'd touched on before, I *was not* 'turned' in the way the legends and lore speak of. The cannibals we'd encountered on the mission trip, I, in essence, became their beverage supply. They'd 'tested' me for virginity, and in finding that to be true, I was deemed a delicacy. They'd kept me alive and around for months, draining yet sustaining me, always their 'vintage' drink for their best meal of the week. And something happened over the course of that time, something that changed me."

"That's horrible," I said.

"I told you," she answered. "There's more, but I'll tell you later. We're almost here."

"Very well," I said as we pulled up to the front of the building. "I *do* want to hear the rest. I mean, it's terrible, I take no pleasure in hearing what happened to you, I just care, and—"

She put her hand on mine, stopping my ramblings and said, "I understand what you mean, no need to explain. *Thank you,* Christopher," she concluded, looking me eye-to-eye and hers beginning to tear just a little. She offered me a strained smile as we stopped and she began to exit the cab.

I looked about for her friend, presuming she'd be there waiting for her. She was not. "Where is your friend?" I asked as Charissa leaned down with the cab door open looking back to me.

"Oh, Ariyah isn't in right now. Saturday night, college town. She's out partying for a while, she'd told me."

"Will you be all right? Do you want me to wait with you until she returns?" I asked.

"Oh no, Christopher." She laughed. "I have a key. Not only has she been there for some good company on occasion but also companionship."

I must have flushed somewhat to that as Charissa giggled at me a little bit more.

"I'm sorry, it appears I've done it again, shared another 'nugget' you're not comfortable with. Your face is very red."

She leaned back further into the cab, giving me a peck on the cheek and concluded, "You're charming. And quite the gentleman, being my escort on the drive. Thank you again, Chris. Let's allow this cabbie to be on his way, and we'll see how things go tomorrow—"

"Tomorrow," I echoed yet another of my growing concerns with her. "You'll be here in the daytime without *your bed.* Will you be all right?"

"You fret overmuch, my friend. Bedroom with closed doors, curtains, and aluminum foil over the windows, I will be perfectly fine. I'm touched, but time for you to go and let this man be on his way," she finished, leaning over the front seatback and giving him his fare.

Transaction completed, she moved out of the car entirely, closing my door, tapping my window, then tapping the front one, signaling the driver to move along. As we pulled away, she waved at me, and I waved back.

The cabbie glanced in his rearview, looking at me. Then he offered me his two cents. "Ya know, Father, if ya ask me, and I know ya didn't, but I'd say that broad wanted ya ta stay 'wit 'er. And hey, even though yer a priest 'n' all, I wouldn't judge ya, notta bit!"

I immediately took his input to heart, embellishing what I'd already been feeling on the drive over. Whatever was happening between us was growing on more than one level. Still, I needed to be strong, keep things in perspective. This bond or whatever the connection was on first a spiritual plane. We at least needed to get through tomorrow before exploring *anything* else. I know I wanted to hear more of her ghastly history, not *just* to empathize or help but because I cared about *her*. No matter how you sliced it, this relationship was getting away from me.

CHAPTER 8

Charissa

I stood there for a time after the cab gone out of sight, reflecting. This man, priest, was able to take me into a dream, talk with me, accompany me, worried about me *after* what I'd done to him. But maybe that was exactly *it.* Could the bite have put him under my spell? It made sense. But if that were true, I was also under his. All he did was annoy me at first; now all he does is stir me. I get teary when I touch his hand and look in his eyes, for Christ's sake!

My reverie was thankfully broken when my phone chimed—a text from Ariyah inviting me to come and join her. She knew my schedule and routine; she *knows me.* Outside of Christopher these last couple of days, she was the only other who was aware of what I am. And though partying was not on the top of my list for activity just now, I *was* here in college town with little else to do until morning.

She was at The Pub, a local watering hole near the university. The text also indicated that she was more than willing to come and pick me up. I messaged her back telling her I was fine to just walk over; running was naturally my first thought but surely not dressed the way I was. And should anyone think to make trouble with me in the night, it would be *they* who would find more trouble than they bargained for.

There was plenty of opportunity for that since the stroll was more than a mile from her place at the Jackson Parkside Apartments. Had I bothered to check my phone prior to the dropoff, I could've had the cabbie take me to The Pub directly. But again, I'd been too distracted by Christopher.

Upon my arrival half an hour later, I descended the steps from the main entryway into the basement, which *was* the whole of the establishment. Ariyah took little time in spotting me once I made my entrance. She ran up, enveloping me in a big, sustained hug. Toward the end of it, I thought she was going to kiss me, but she hesitated briefly and passed on it. I knew why. I detected the scent of a man on her and my keen sense of smell also picked up that he was present and not far away. I suspected she didn't want to complicate whatever she had cooking with him by making a spectacle kissing me. And that was perfect for me with how I'd been feeling toward Christopher. Any intimacy with another, especially the same sex, struck me as highly inappropriate.

We broke our clinch, looking at one another with a sharp clarity of where we were at with each other, an unspoken understanding. I suppose it was why I'd chosen Ariyah as a confidant and a friend. She had that way of reading me, getting me without much conversation required. I attributed this to my sense of her as an old soul. I think she'd gained at least *some* of that from her travels abroad after high school. She was slightly older than your average college student as she was one those who'd done the European backpacking routine instead of going straight onto her higher education. Those journeys had included going to my homeland of England as well, thus, another key connection between us. It was a natural segue for her to visit there, as she was a native of the Bahamas, a British territory. Undoubtedly the less inhibited European sexual culture also contributed to her exploration of pleasure and pain with me.

She then took me to the table where she and her friends were at, including the boy of her interest. And I do say "boy," as he *was* your average college age. I had to refrain from a slight hunger pang; he looked like a thoroughly luscious little snack! Ariyah, catching this, furrowed her brow at me, putting me back in check. Good thing I hadn't ordered any wine yet. Though the introductions had gone well (his name was Joe), it was at that point she decided to pull me away from there and go to the dance floor.

Once we got our bodies moving, we were in sync as usual. We both glanced back at our table to Joe and the group. We caught the stares toward us, Joe's in particular. And then for some reason, we just laughed aloud about it. At that point we sustained the vocal level of the laughter, shouting out some conversation over the music as we danced. Amidst our chatter, I'd told her I'd met a priest and she said that she was going to church for Easter with Joe in the morning. She'd gone on to say she was planning on going home with him tonight, asking me if I still had my key.

Hearing this, I immediately dragged her off the dance floor and led her over to the bar. I was as surprised at my sudden reaction as she. "Ariyah, dear," I began, "unless you've had a secret wedding you neglected to mention, you *cannot* go home with Joe tonight, then turn right around and go to Easter Sunday Mass like that! It's not right." I was as shocked as she at what had just poured out of my mouth. So conservative, so puritanical, so Catholic. *So* not me. At least not the me of the present. But certainly the me of the past. Once more, this *had* to have something to do with Christopher.

Equally surprising was the answer that was forthcoming from her. After she'd defensively pointed out they were going to a Protestant church, not a Catholic Mass, she continued, "You're absolutely right! That *would* be so wrong, now that you mention it. How long did you say you've been hanging out with this priest?"

"Only two days," I answered. "But I bit him. And I comingled our blood, *mine* over his bite wound to heal it so he wouldn't know when I blanked out his memory of it. But he figured it out from dreams he started having of me, Christ and blood. It's all unraveling, Ari. It's why I came tonight. We're *so* connected, he and I, with dreams and visions. I'm fearful about tomorrow and what it might be like. I came here to get out of my neighborhood, get some distance between he and I while he does bloody *triple* masses!"

"Oh my god," she said, putting her hand on mine. "Do you want me to *not* go with Joe in the morning and stay home with you? I'm totally there for you if you need me."

"No, go," I said. "Go with Joe. I simply need the distance your residence provides and to be alone. I just have to sleep and get through the morning is all. I'll be fine."

"All right, if you're sure," she replied. "But I *do* think it's time to bail and have Joe take us home now. If you don't want me with you tomorrow, let me at least keep you company through tonight. Besides, I want to catch up with you, not spend all night here getting drunk. *That* won't do me much good in the morning anyway."

"Agreed," I said.

*****

Joe had dropped us off at the front of her building at about eleven. Early by Saturday evening standards but ladies' choice. Not only was Joe disappointed Ariyah hadn't gone home with him, he was likely let down at not being invited up, with all possibilities of the company of *two* women on his mind.

As we rode the elevator up to her fourth floor flat, I leaned into her to give the greeting kiss that never happened earlier. It was soft, affectionate but brief. We'd missed each other. I backed off, taking her hands to mine.

"That's all for tonight," I told her. "For now, I have my priest, you have your Joe. While they are with us, it should be no more. Just talk with me."

"Perfect," she replied. "I think Joe was bummed on two counts: me not going home with him *and* him not up here *with* us. Serves him right, though. He's the one who invited me to church."

As the elevator chimed and let us out, we walked on as I continued, "If I may say, the notion of being at the bar late and then church in the morning doesn't really equate."

"Oh yeah," she said. "That was our classmates' idea. I'm not one for that as much as they are, but what the heck. It was the end of the term, and the work's been hard. Joe wasn't going to miss it."

"Well, I've *missed* you," I said, putting my arm around her with a good squeeze as we approached the door. Once inside, we chatted for a while longer until I realized it was past midnight. I told her she needed rest for morning.

"What about you?" she asked. "You've got till dawn before you sleep—"

"I need to prepare the guest room against the sun. Afterward I can drink some wine if you have any and curl up with a book. I'll be fine."

"If you say so. Good night then."

I took her face in my hands, pecked her on the lips, kissed her forehead, told her thank you, and said good night.

Christopher

Sleep was always a difficult prospect for a priest on the eve of Easter Sunday, much like children on Christmas Eve. But it was not the anticipation of presents I was keyed up over before I finally went down. It was the anxiousness of what might loom for Charissa and I this morning as the masses would begin.

My dreams had been a little less vivid than the previous night, though still strangely curious. I'd seen two of the Marys again; they'd been consoling each other, likely over their loss of Jesus. Their embrace sustained for a time, and it became more passionate as they then morphed into Charissa and another woman, presumably her friend Ariyah. Same-sex relations never failed to baffle me. They ceased their carrying on when a triad of figures entered the dream. One was a college-aged young man; another, myself; and the third, the Lord. Both women becoming aware of these presences and moved apart from each other—Ariyah going to the lad, Charissa coming to me, and both nodding to Jesus.

I imagine the remembrance of the dream had turned into something of a daydream as I found myself distracted by it while I conducted the first mass the next morning. But that was nothing compared to what I would experience once we'd begun serving Communion. As parishioners started chewing their pieces of bread, I pictured Charissa biting everyone. Upon the taking of the wine, it turned ghastly. She was like an alcoholic at a wine tasting, sampling more blood than she could physically consume. Her normally beautiful face was covered in the stuff, as if from the back spray of a gun fired at someone at close range.

At the close of the Mass I was seriously rattled. Like any server at a restaurant, I'd kept my best face forward, smiling and greeting as if nothing were wrong. Once everyone was dispersed from first service, I took a break before those lined up for the second started in. I needed to pray for myself, for Charissa, and for my people here today that they'd not be affected by any residual behavior on my part to these strange circumstances. Because, based on what I'd already seen from only *one* Mass, I didn't honestly know how I was going to make it through two more.

*****

The second Mass commenced. It went well enough from opening through liturgy but went wrong again as the Lord's Supper was served. This time, as the bread elements were offered, I saw Charissa in her dominatrix garb parading around with platters like a waitress, with body parts on the plates upon her trays. She had pieces of flesh on the corners of her mouth and under her chin. She had a look about her like she'd truly grown full already but was at an all-you-can-eat buffet and just had to keep going.

Then came the wine. I could barely distinguish the beverage within the cups from the deluge of blood I was seeing in my vision. It spilled all over from goblets on Charissa's tray. She finally just heaved the platter into the air, becoming unholy grails reigning blood everywhere. She stood there, arms spread open wide like someone dancing in the rain while crimson washed over her.

And if this weren't already terrifying enough, it then became *really* bizarre. Charissa stood tall in front of everyone, in that spot that was the break in the pews. She looked around with blood all over her, simultaneously appearing very, *very* full. She looked nauseous and started coughing. Then she began to dry heave. And next came the vomiting. She spewed out blood in a quantity equal to what she'd drunk, reminiscent of an anorexic. But it didn't stop there. After the blood came water. *Water!* Like Christ when he died. Blood and water.

I looked at her, or the vision I was having of her, that is. I saw that as the water gurgled out of her mouth, she looked as if she was drowning—full, vomiting, drowning. There was some connection to these things, just like there was significance to water following blood when Jesus died. I just needed to figure out what it was. And I had to do it fast because I was suddenly getting the distinct feeling that Charissa—the *real* her and not this vision—was in trouble right now, just like this troubling imagery was showing me.

There was no way of knowing what could be going on with her at this moment, but I wouldn't find out by remaining here. God knew by the time a third Mass was performed, things could be critical. It was time to get someone to sub for me and get back out to Woodlawn.

CHAPTER 9

Charissa

Once I'd awoke from the awful dream of my darting through the congregation and biting them, there would be no going back to sleep. So much for my distance here in Woodlawn making a difference. I was sweaty, like after a run, and thirsty, too, even though the amount I'd drunk in the dream should have had me feeling full.

After I washed my face, I returned to my darkened room, still jittery. I was feeling foolish now, for telling Ariyah to go, that I'd be fine on my own. I wasn't. Probably her being out *doing* the very act from the dream, communion, was adding to my stress. Having been intimate with her, I was likely picking up on her participation in the activity as well. *Cursed*, I thought. I am truly cursed. If God were doing some work in me through this, I'd have to say "it felt like the devil," to coin a phrase.

I tried thinking of Christopher, *only* Chris—not his priestliness, not serving the meal, not biting, him, just him. I tried picturing running with him, riding in the cab with him, talking with him. And it worked. I calmed down and eased my worried mind. Not to the point of returning back to slumber, mind you, but at least relaxed—enough to skirt the edges of rest anyway.

Good thing, too, for the next wave of dream would not be suppressed, even if I *was* awake. In the next onslaught of imagery, I was not only consuming blood like a ravenous pack animal, but also, I was eating the flesh of people too, akin to the cannibals I was borne of. I was a glutton who would not stop. My eyes were closed, and I was practically tearing my hair out to try and stop the visions, but they would *not* go away.

Finally, I began reacting physically to it all. I was feeling like an amateur in a hot dog eating competition, gagging and ready to puke. And I did. Being that my diet *is* blood, that is what came out in what seemed like gallons! Luckily I'd made it to the bathroom before the bloodbath ensued and not making Ariyah's guestroom look like a murder scene. As the flow began to slow, *that* gave me an idea. *Blood, bath. Bath, room.* For some reason, probably this psychic backlash from Christopher's Mass, I thought of the spear piercing Christ's side and the blood *and* water pouring forth.

I scampered to the bathtub and started filling it up, a towel to my mouth for the blood still seeping out. I shut my eyes in prayer, trying to call forth the Charissa of old who served the church dutifully those centuries ago. I combined *that* with my bond to the priest, doing my best to *bless* this water rising in the tub. Once it was full, I disrobed and settled in to immerse myself under it. Finally, I did what would kill a normal human in an act that I'd hoped would somehow heal me of this ill. I breathed it in.

Ariyah

Joe and I were returning from the midmorning church service we'd gone to. He'd wanted to go directly for brunch, but I told him no, that we needed to stop home first and check on Charissa. I had a bad feeling; I'd had it since Communion at the end. I'd experienced some racing thoughts of her and blood and biting. When I'd glanced briefly at the pastor here and there, I'd envisioned a Catholic priest, no doubt some notion of her Christopher.

And that was *exactly* who appeared getting out of a cab in the front of my building as we got there. "Father Christopher?" I asked.

"I am," he said. "Ariyah, I presume?"

"The same," I answered. "This is Joe. Joseph Vollen, my...boyfriend." I was surprised at how the introduction came out; we weren't fully established as *that,* but it was what escaped my lips. Joe smiled at me, surprised as well but apparently happy about it.

"I'm sorry," began the Father, "but I thought you and Charissa *were—*"

"Y'know, I kinda had that vibe about them, too, Father," said Joe.

"Guys!" I snapped. "We're here to check on *her*, aren't we? Father, you wouldn't *be* here if you didn't think something was off with her, am I right? I know that's why I've come home early. Let's get upstairs now, please!"

The Father took no more prompting than that, but Joe, looking befuddled, needed my hand pulling him forward to get him going.

Once on the elevator, awkward though it was, I turned to Christopher semi privately and asked in a whisper, "You *know* about her, right? She told me she bit you, so I'm assuming—"

"She did, and I *do*. Know, that is. Does Joseph?" he whispered back.

I shook my head no.

Christopher nodded at me affirmatively, as we all got out on my floor, hurrying toward the apartment, with Joe looking at us curiously from our exchange. As I pulled out my key to unlock the door, I pulled Joe close.

"Hon," I began quietly, "Charissa has some unique issues, which the Father and I know about. We're both pretty sure that she may be having a problem in there, so let us take the lead, and you kinda keep back, okay?"

"Uh, sure," he answered with growing apprehension.

We entered, and everything looked fine at first. As we got to the hallway toward the bedrooms, we saw spots of blood leading from the guestroom to the bathroom. The door was closed. As I'd suggested, Joe stayed back at the perimeter of living room to the hall, but Christopher was moving fast to open the bathroom door.

I stepped in front of him and reminded, "*If* she's not decent in there, I'd better go first, don't you think, *Father?*"

"Yes, of course," he replied, suddenly embarrassed.

I went in, and spying Charissa naked in the bathtub, I quickly closed the door behind me. She was curled up, practically fetal, in a draining tub of pinkish water.

"Hello, my friend," she said groggily, turning to look at me.

I moved toward her and knelt down to the tub's rim, taking her hand.

"Oh honey," I began, "what happened?"

"*You* happened," she answered. "You and him. He's here with you, isn't he? Both of your participations in communion this morning have wreaked havoc on me. *You* from our bond of having been together, and *he* from the blood share I stupidly performed."

"I get that," I said. "I've 'seen' things in my head of you earlier. It's why I rushed back here. But what *is* this? Why are you lying in the bathtub? Is this your blood in the water?"

"It's," she replied with pause, coughing, "a *mix* of all the blood I've vomited and the bathwater. I thought to try and 'bless' it as best I could, making it 'holy water.' Then I breathed it in, in hopes of purging my system. I knew it wouldn't kill me because…well, you *know*."

"My god, Charissa, I knew you might be in trouble, but I had no idea it was this bad," I cried.

"Help me up, will you please?" she asked. "I'm *so* weak and drained. If Christopher is here, and he's willing, I'm going to need him. But I have to get dressed."

"Of course," I said, helping her up. As she rose in her obvious exhaustion, an odd parallel crossed my mind, one I never would have thought of if today wasn't Easter. What Jesus went through in sacrifice for mankind, I saw a glimpse of it in front of me in Charissa's pinkish waterlogged naked body. Something horrible she'd just endured over *us*, me and this priest, and our connection to her. And *only because* of that union. I felt a humbling and an awareness that suddenly overwhelmed me emotionally.

I leaned into her and hugged her hard. She tried to hug me back with equal force, but it just wasn't in her. Normally, she could squeeze the life out of *me.* As she started to slip and lose her footing, I surged up and supported her. Then I set her down to sit on the tub's rim, putting a towel over her shoulders.

I turned to the door and said, "Excuse me, dear, I'm going to get you a robe so you're presentable, okay?"

Charissa nodded, still clearly dazed.

When I reached the hall closet, passing by Christopher, I told him, "I'm getting her a robe so she's decent. She needs *you,* and I'll bet you know what for. She's in bad shape, and it's due to both of us, where we've been doing you know what this morning. I'm going back to dress her, then you can go in. She's too weak to walk her around right now. I'll be back in a sec, then give you two some privacy."

He nodded as I went back in to take care of her. Charissa looked up at me smiling as I reentered. "Here you go, honey," I said, helping her into the robe.

"Thank you," she said, sitting back down with a sigh. "I probably should have had you stay with me this morning."

"Damn straight you should have," I said. "Having me out in church, doing the same thing Christopher was only multiplied whatever this is you went through. I think you'll be staying here with me for a while, dear."

She nodded and said, "For more reasons than you might have concluded. I *may* have to do this again at a place not far from here. But I'll talk to you about that later. If you don't mind, I'm ready for Christopher to come in now please."

"Of course," I said, curious about her mysterious pronouncement just then. "I'll go get him now."

CHAPTER 10

Christopher

I went in, sitting down next to Charissa and said immediately, "I'm *so* sorry," not even asking what had happened to her. To me, it was fairly clear.

"Not as sorry as I am," she answered, laying her head on my shoulder. "I began this, after all."

"Yes, but I *invited* it," I returned.

"Fine," she answered. "We're equally to blame then. Recriminations aside, I have need of you *now,* Christopher. Are you willing?" she asked looking at me with tired eyes, pleading.

Honestly, I was highly uncertain. I knew what she was asking. She needed blood, and because of this bizarre link between us now, I suspected she required mine, specifically. What could I do? Refuse her? After my worry had driven me all the way here from Old Town? Abandoning my people for the third Mass to come be with her? No, I could not.

Seated together as we were, I simply sighed and slowly craned my neck to the side opposite her, removing my collar. She slithered her head into my neck, nuzzling me. I was more than sustenance to her at this point; she cared too.

She whispered to me softly, "Thank you," then bit and dug in.

Strangely, though the initial pinch of her fangs were like the needle of a blood draw, what followed was extraordinary. Maybe it was on account of all the focus to the taking of the cup from earlier; maybe it was due to the blood bond that we now shared. In any case, the concept of transubstantiation had never come to me clearer. As I felt my blood flowing into her mouth, I also felt the strength she drew from it, not merely the taking of what is a normal meal for her but even more so the "Christ in *me*" renewing her spirit. I literally sensed the light of the world brightening her darkened soul. It was utterly magical, even if what it looked like to the naked eye appeared ghastly. I'd daresay this could be what the experience of Communion was truly meant to be, after a fashion, of course.

Her utter depletion was crystal clear as she drank deeply, simultaneously holding onto my shoulder with a vice grip. It was as if she were a baby on her mother's breast. Perhaps it was the intensity of her feeding or the euphoria I was experiencing as she did; but at some point, I must've been smacking my hand on the tub rim itself, as if we were throes of lovemaking. I suspect it was this racket that brought Ariyah bolting into the room to see what might be wrong.

"Dammit, Charissa! Enough!" she shouted. She moved to us and knelt down, trying to ease Charissa off me. As Ariyah gently removed her so as not to rip my throat out, she looked to me and said, "Sorry, Father, pardon my cursing, I apologize. I just wanted to make sure she didn't drink *all* of you."

"It's all right," I said, craning and wiping off my neck. "I should've been paying more attention to how long she was drinking myself, but I think I went somewhere else while she was."

"It can happen," said Charissa, wiping her mouth as I had my neck. "When there's more to it than meal, when two are allied as we are, it can be a little intense, and paying heed to the duration can get away from you. It's why I've *never* drank from Ariyah when we've been together."

"Really?" asked Ariyah, surprised. "Now that you mention it, you're right! I can't remember you biting me except for in a session."

I stopped them both right there. "Ariyah," I said, looking at them *both,* "the cursing is excusable, but what goes on between the two of you *is* more than I need to hear. Excuse me." I started up to exit the room. By the time I reached the door, both women were on either side of me, helping me through. Apparently, I was lightheaded and woozy from blood loss.

Charissa looked up at me with sad eyes, feeling guilty over it no doubt, patting my shoulder. "Thank you, ladies," I said while nuzzling my head to Charissa's briefly.

"Get him on the couch," said Ariyah. "I'll go get some juice and fruit to help him replenish."

"Replenish what?" Joe asked from his living room seat where he'd opted to occupy himself watching a Cubs game.

"Nothing, sweetheart," Ariyah answered, rummaging through the refrigerator. "He's a little tired from doing all the masses this morning, plus coming all the way over here. I'm just getting him a bite and a drink."

Good answer, I thought. Ironically amusing too—*a bite and a drink.* I'm not sure he bought it entirely, considering the to-do we made when we first got here. But at least the attention was now deferred from Charissa to me.

"Speaking of a bite," Joe continued, "if you guys are all good here, whaddya say me n' you go get, well, I guess it's *lunch* by now," to Ariyah.

To which she gave a look to kill, perceiving him to have been rude to Charissa and I. Charissa immediately nodded affirmatively to her, enthusiastically even, I'd say. Getting Joe out of here and away from asking more questions awkward to answer was a grand idea.

Moments thereafter, I was served some apple slices and orange juice with Joe and Ariyah quickly out the door. In the wake of their departure, Charissa and I simply fell into each other in relief that we'd potentially avoided and what we'd just gotten through.

Charissa

We both just sat there on the couch for a bit while the Cubs game continued on the television. I put my hand on Christopher's and asked, "How are you feeling now?"

"Better," he said.

"I can't thank you enough for that, for feeding me. I'm sorry I got carried away. I felt half dead. Nothing like that has ever happened to me before, and I've been around awhile."

"Just *how* long have you lived, Charissa?" asked Christopher.

"About two hundred and fifty years, give or take." Then I laughed thinking about my age and the ballgame on the TV in the background. "I *did* see when the Cubs won their first pennant!"

Then Christopher laughed too. This was good. The morning had been far too horrific and serious. We needed this. *We.* Was I actually referring to ourselves in the plural now? After two days? My god.

Chris then thankfully interrupted. "Charissa, if I may ask, why did you wait to drink of me when Ariyah saw to you first?"

"I most certainly would have had you not been here. But given that you were, I felt like I didn't need to risk the possibility of strengthening the link with yet another. What I'd picked up from *her* this morning was minimal compared to you. Since I don't see how the bond between *us* could get more damaging than it already is, I went with you. Plus I think God *is* working on me in this, and it is clearly through *you.*"

"As you'd brought up before," Chris reminded. "If you don't mind my asking, given you've embellished the point again, *how* do you see Him doing so?"

"Well, one thing has certainly come to mind since we've been sitting here. Have you noticed? It's *daytime,* and the drapes in here are *not* closed. We're getting direct sunlight, and so far, I've been okay. I'm not feeling sick, no rash, boils, anything. We were all so keyed up when we got in here it escaped my notice at first. But since they've left, I surely *have* noted it, and look at me! I'm fine!"

"You certainly are, it appears," he said. "So you're saying you think the Lord is taking away your vampirism?"

"I'm saying that it's a start. I clearly still need blood sustenance, as our time in the bathroom just proved. But I don't know. While I was in the water, before you all returned, as I breathed it in, I had vision of being in another body of water close by here. Do you know of where I speak? It is significant in name."

"I might, but back up, please. You just said you breathed water into yourself? From the bathtub? Were you trying to kill yourself?"

"No no, not at all. I'm sorry, I forgot. I told Ariyah, not you. I had the notion to attempt flushing all the blood vomit out of my system with 'holy water.' I'd drawn upon my connection to you *and* the church servant I once was in an attempt to bless the water I'd filled up the tub with."

"That's why I had a vision of you drowning!" Chris exclaimed.

"Yes, but I *can't* drown. Anyway, there's your explanation for all of that. So the vision I had while in the water and 'purging,' I was in the lagoon in the Garden of the Phoenix." I paused there in attempt to let that hang for dramatic effect, to see if it would strike him in the same way it had occurred to me. It took him a moment, but he got it.

"I see," he said, puzzled at first. But then, "Oh! *I see!*" he exclaimed. "A parallel to *you* being *as* a phoenix rising from your own ashes! The idea has some merit. But how did you know that's where you were in the vision?"

"Good point," I agreed. "When I came up out of the bathwater here, I saw myself rising from the water in the visualization, and I recognized the place. Having spent time with Ariyah here previously, we've been there. So I believe this is telling me something."

"Telling you *what,* precisely? To go and 'purge' yourself again *there?"*

"Perhaps," I answered. "I don't think I want to go running over there just now to test the theory. I've had enough of that for one day already."

"Good," he agreed. "I don't think I've got enough left in me to 'donate' twice in one day either."

And *we* laughed together again.

CHAPTER 11

Ariyah

By the time I got back, calling it a day with Joe, Charissa and Christopher were *still* there on the couch talking. I couldn't believe it; I'd been gone an hour and a half myself!

"Hi, guys," I said. "Thanks a lot for having me deal with more of Joe's questions by myself."

Charissa looked at me sideways and said bluntly, "We needed to get him out of here, and he gave us the perfect opening by wanting to go get lunch with you. What else should we have done?"

"No, it's all right," I said. "I'm just messing with you. When he pressed more about it, I simply told him you're agoraphobic and mildly schizophrenic."

"Thanks a lot," she said. "Touché."

"Hey," I began, "have you two seriously just been sitting here in the same spot talking all this time?"

"No," said Christopher, finally adding his own two cents. "We actually both fell asleep for a little bit. It wasn't hard for *her.* She's normally sleeping now anyway."

"Yeah, no doubt." I laughed. "Wait a minute!" I exclaimed, noticing the drapes open in a room with Charissa in it, in the daytime! "What's up with *this?* Are you out of your mind, Charissa?"

"Look at me, Ariyah," she replied stoically. "Does it look like it's affecting me?"

"Actually, no, it doesn't. You look fine. How's that possible?"

"I don't know, honestly. For now, let's chalk it up to keeping company with this 'good shepherd.' Speaking of which, I was just starting to tell him more of my origin story."

"I know that tale," I said.

"Not *all* of it, you don't," Charissa declared. "Come, sit down with us while I tell you the rest of the story."

"Proceed, Paula Harvey," joked Christopher.

"All right," began Charissa. "You both know how my mission trip to the West Indies brought us unwittingly into a tribe of cannibals and how they used me to drink from for months on end. But that alone wasn't *entirely* what turned me. As I've said, I was the 'fine wine' for the tribes' family meal each week. There came a point when there was some special celebration that lasted over the course of several days like an extended holiday weekend we might observe in our civilized countries. During that period, they'd drained me utterly. They'd gotten careless, and I believe I literally *died.*

"When they'd realized what they'd done, draining their precious virgin 'drink' to death, they weren't having it. They'd sought out a medicine man, witch doctor, whatever you want to call him from a neighboring tribe, as they did not have one of their own. It wasn't a clan they were on the best of terms with. It was akin to relations between Russia and America during the Cold War. The other tribe had their own reasons for offering the aid, as I'd find out later.

"Anyway, this shaman came in, performed magics upon me, and I believe gave me his own blood in order to somehow revive my essence. It worked obviously, but I clearly wasn't the same. I'd become as he was—some kind of cannibal-vampire hybrid. And once the change occurred, it was clear why he'd done it for them. Not to aid them but to destroy them. Once I'd transformed into this unholy thing, I went on a rampage throughout the village, killing and drinking everyone I could.

"My months of bondage to them, the slaughter and consumption of my people, it all came out in a murderous rage that wouldn't stop until I'd slain all of them who didn't get away. Ariyah, you'd fibbed to Joseph about my being schizophrenic, but I acted every bit as one. *Absolutely* psychotic I daresay."

"My god, Chris," I cried.

"Oh, it gets better, Ariyah, believe me. Once that was all over, I'd decided I was going to go back to England and seek vengeance upon those who'd sent us, no matter how long it took me."

"Before you get into that," I interrupted, playing unconsciously with the pendant on my necklace. "Let's camp out at that part about the cannibal-vampire-shaman guy. There's something familiar about that, a tale I've heard in island lore about such a man. I take it you didn't kill him too?"

"No, I never found him again. It's hard to say how I feel about him. Part of me hates him for making me *this.* Turning me into a weapon to unleash on his rivals, not to mention all the other killing I've done since. On the other hand, he gave me life again, and it hasn't been all bad."

"Regardless, Charissa," I jumped back in, diddling again with the pendant. "This vamp-shaman dude could be more than a myth. The tall tales of him go on to this day. I've grown up in the Bahamas hearing them, and I don't mind telling you that I've always stayed well clear of the isles he's purported to be in. Most of the locals consider it to be urban, well, I guess that would be *suburban* legend, huh! Even so, people make it a point to avoid there."

"That's amazing, Ariyah," said Charissa riveted. "I'm surprised I've never heard of any of this."

"Perhaps the fact that you're hearing about it now," began Christopher, "*is* a sign within this process of what God is doing in you."

"A sign of what?" asked Charissa.

"Well, if Christ's nature is indeed overcoming your vampirism, it could be a clue to go seek him out and forgive him, if these stories she speaks of are true and he still lives."

"Are you kidding?" I blasted, now fisting my pendant. "Why the hell would she do that?"

"No, he's right," Charissa replied. "I *am* feeling more of a godlike nature flowing through me, especially since my meal of Christopher. And *that* would be a natural progression if 'this phoenix is going to rise.'"

"Huh?" I asked, confused. "What's *that* about?"

"You recall I told you of maybe needing to do what I did in the bathtub again? What I'd tell you more of later? Well, when I was under, I had a vision of being submerged in the Garden of the

Phoenix, right near here. I feel like it might necessary to do again, I don't know—"

"*Rinse and repeat,* you're saying, Chris?" I joked, curious to her meaning.

Father Christopher once more had some "fatherly" wisdom to add and said, "That's a good metaphor, Ariyah. In our walks with God, we are in constant cycles of repenting and then *cleansing* our sins through the blood of Christ. So in essence, wash, *rinse, repeat.*"

"Okay," I said sarcastically, "so, is she supposed to go and 'drown' herself every time she feeds now or something?"

"Impossible to say," he began in answer, "the Lord will have to reveal His intent to her. *That* would seem to me to be redundant and counterproductive, actually."

"Kind of in the same way going after the shaman strikes me, counterproductive," I said.

"Well, I think I'm going to do it," Charissa said. "Go after him, that is."

We all paused for a moment following her declaration, looking about at each other, stunned. Then I said it: "Well, I for one, am *not* going anywhere near that place, and I don't think you should either."

"Christopher, how about you?" Charissa asked, eyeing him intently.

"Well," he began, "it is certainly not something at the top of my bucket list. But since it seems I'm becoming something of your escort of late, *yes,* I would consider accompanying you."

"I think you're both insane," I said, looping the necklace chain around my finger nervously.

Christopher

Charissa walked me downstairs, as at this point, I was well overdue to return. She'd borrowed a hoodie from Ariyah, in case the direct sun, beyond indoors, proved to be a problem. As she'd already said, she was going to stay on with her friend for a while, who opted to remain inside.

"So you're serious?" I asked. "About seeking out the shaman?"

"I know it sounds impulsive," she returned. "But I'm not kidding about this 'God connection' that's happening to me. And your take on going to forgive him, *if* he still exists, makes some sense to me."

"If forgiveness to the man is sounding logical to you, I'd say, yes, God is truly beginning to flow into you," commented Christopher.

"Don't get me wrong, Chris," she began, "I don't know that I'm feeling it through my *entire* being yet. I still have a lot of anger toward him—*all* the cannibals, if I'm honest. Though I had my revenge, that's really only ever a bandage. Some things you never really get over."

We walked out of and past the elevators, through the lobby, and toward the building's front doors. As we did, Charissa laid a hand upon my shoulder and continued, "You know, the forgiveness aspect isn't the *only* thing that has an impact on me. While I was feeding on you, holding your shoulder like I am now, I felt something else as well. Between the touch *and* the blood, I felt my spirit go elsewhere. As though I were tapping into God's source, essence, whatever you want to call it. *Away* from *this* plane is what I'm trying to say. And it was predicated by my closeness to you in that moment."

I didn't know quite what to say as I held the door open for her and we went out. I experienced everything she was saying as well, but as a priest, I was still struggling with the appropriateness of this entire situation. The feeding, the touching, lounging together on the couch—not exactly how I'm supposed to behave with a woman. And yet…

"Cat got your tongue, my priest?" she queried, snapping her fingers first to my face, then repeating the gesture, raising her arm to hail a cab.

"I'm at odds, Charissa," I said with pause. "It is this blood and mental bond. To say nothing of the one I think we're *both* feeling as a man and a woman. From my particular position, it's a lot."

"I understand," she replied. "I was wondering which of us would be brave enough to speak of *that* first. I've wanted to say something but was uncertain whether to or not. It's good that it came from you."

"Thanks, I think," I replied.

"You know what *I think?*" she asked, then answered, "I believe we should both step back a little and ponder things. *You* go back to your church and your people, and with this Easter fiasco behind us, just get back to some normalcy. I'll stay here a couple of days with Ariyah and just relax, think things through."

"That sounds like an excellent idea," I returned.

"Then," she continued, "perhaps we could meet up for run in a few days and see where we're at."

"Agreed," I said.

"How about I give you a dream call and see how well we're still dialed up after a couple of days?" she questioned.

"I suppose that would be all right," I said, "or if that doesn't work, do it the old-fashioned way and just call me at the church."

"Very well," she concluded as a cab pulled up.

We paused looking to each other, debating, I suspect, *how* we should part—simply a goodbye, a hug, or *more* than that, God forbid.

With the cabbie waiting, pressing us to a decision, Charissa said finally, "To hell with it," and compressed herself into me. It was a heartfelt, tender embrace in which I heard her whisper "thank you" quietly. I don't know if it was to me or to God, perhaps both. Either way, when we pulled away from each other, her eyes mirrored affection to me and God's love together in unison. She smiled, as did I, then winked as I got in the cab.

CHAPTER 12

Charissa

After I'd watched Christopher drive away, I decided to linger outside for a little bit, to further test how I was doing out of doors in the daytime. Though it *was* overcast, it was nonetheless daylight—an entirely new dynamic for me. I paced the block outside the apartment complex briefly, keeping the hoodie over my head for good measure. I *was* enjoying it, but I wasn't about to be a fool and parade around unprotected like a bloke *singin' in the rain.*

After a while, as things appeared to be all right, I stepped up to the side of a building and removed my phone from my pocket to call Ariyah. When she picked up, I said, "Hi, honey, I'm done, and Christopher is off on his way. I'm doing okay so far in the daylight, so I was wondering if you'd like to come down and we could go for a walk?"

There was pause with a sigh, as though she still thought my sanity was slipping. Finally she said, "I guess so, Chris. It seems like you're pushing it to me, but at least if I join you, there'll be someone watching out for you. Please tell me you're keeping the hoodie on."

"Yes, Mother," I replied sarcastically. "I *may* be pushing the envelope, but I'm not an imbecile. Tell you what, I'll circle back and meet you in your building's lobby."

"All right, Chris," she replied. "I'll see you in five."

*****

Ten minutes later, we were again joined together and walking toward the Garden of the Phoenix in Jackson Park. Ariyah had not truly been paying attention to the direction we were headed, as I believe she was too distracted by my traversing in the light. She kept watching me, monitoring for any sign of my falling ill. Thus, by the time the park was in sight, she was taken by surprise. But only for a moment.

"Oh," said Ariyah. "So *this* is our destination. I might've guessed if I'd noticed which way we were going. You're here for a reason, no doubt. Please tell me you're not planning to drown yourself again."

"No," I said, laughing. "Like I told Chris, that's *not* repeating anymore today. Never again would be too soon, but there *is* that vision to explore. I just want to walk around, see if I get any impressions, that's all. Just pretend we're taking a stroll in the park like we have before."

"Okay," she answered, taking my hand. "As long as that's a promise, we need to just chill for the rest of the day. In fact, make that for as long as you decide to hang around."

"Yes, ma'am, my host, it will be as you say," I answered, to which we both laughed heartily between ourselves. It was good to laugh after all of the madness of the morning. But it *would not* be "as she said." Just as I had when I'd joined Christopher for his ceremony in the very beginning, I'd prove myself just as foolhardy as then very shortly.

As we crossed the Japanese moon bridge over the koi pond, I'd decided to hike up my pants and wet my feet in the lagoon.

"What are you—" Ariyah started to ask, playing the mother hen role to the hilt. Once she saw that all I was doing was simply standing and walking slowly about in the shallows, she pulled the claws back in. As it turned out though, she *was* right in her apprehension after all.

Once it appeared that I was getting nothing by way of any impressions to my earlier vision of here, I slipped headlong into a very stupid move, unthinking. I pulled the hoodie down, outstretched my arms and looked up into the sky. Then I closed my eyes and circle-stepped around where I was standing, seeking to prompt my vision to elaborate itself somehow. I think I may had been starting to get something, but before I could achieve any clarity, I suddenly felt nauseous and dizzy.

As I began to waver, losing my equilibrium, Ariyah was upon me, holding and steadying me.

"Did I *not* tell you that someone's gotta watch after you?" she said, scolding. "I thought you told me you *weren't* an idiot. Seems like you're acting like one to me. What was *that* all about? And *why the hell* would you look directly up at the sun? You moron!"

"Sorry," I said as she hoisted me up out of the water and quickly led me over to the shade of a nearby Japanese maple tree. "So I *am* an idiot as it turns out. I lost my focus while trying to prod my vision to come back."

"So you go and look straight up into sky to do so," she replied curtly. "Brilliant. You know, *just* because you might be in some kind of transition, let me remind you, *you're* still *a vampire,* Charissa! You're supposed to be indoors right now at the very least, resting and sleeping comfortably at most! But *what* are you doing instead? Walking outside with me in a park, a considerable distance from home, and now you're getting sick. What am I going to do with you?"

"Stay with me under this tree perhaps, until dusk settles in," I answered. "How about that? I think I'll be all right till then—"

"You bet I'll be right here with you! God knows if I left, you'd get yourself into more trouble," she returned with a sigh.

"Normally," I began in reply, "I would remind you who's the dominant and who's the submissive here, but considering my behavior today, I suspect I deserve all your mothering."

"Damn straight," she answered. "I have some water in my bag, do you need some?"

"Yes, thank you," I said. After I guzzled the bottle down, I wiped my mouth and sighed.

"Do you need anything *stronger?*" she queried, barring me her wrist. "I'll trust you *not* to be the glutton you were with Christopher—"

"All right," I said, "I could use a little, I imagine, thanks."

I was very cautious at this point to police myself closely, only having what would constitute as an appetizer. I definitely made sure *not* to use any of my own blood to heal the bite wound, for fear of creating another bonding "monster" neither of us needed.

It was odd feeding upon her outside the context of a session with me. And ironically enough, she asked me if we could have one again soon, perhaps joining me on my return home in a few days. I think she sensed that our physical relationship with each other was waning, as we both had gentlemen in our lives now. I'd never had intention to involve myself intimately with another woman, but she'd become a friend, we'd both been lonely I suspect, and one thing had led to another. I've never been one who felt relations between the same sex was at all appropriate in the first place, being originally Catholic myself. Then again, with the blood I've spilled and the work I do, one might say I've strayed considerably.

Regardless, the couple of hours we spent there under the tree passed quickly enough. We'd talked of many things—Christopher and Joseph, both of our experiences in Europe, and so on and so forth, as women will. At some point, I think I'd fallen asleep with my head in her lap, as she'd nudged me awake sometime later, letting me know it was finally dusk.

"Wakey-wakey, day sleeper," joked Ariyah. "All better now? Ready to go home?"

"I suppose," I answered, feeling a little off. "I feel like I'm experiencing jet lag or something, being awake in the daytime. It's strange."

"Well," she began, pulling me up. "Your natural sleep schedule certainly caught up with you just now I'd say. Hey, did you dream while you slept? Get anything like from your vision that you were after?"

"Perhaps," I said. "Nothing like before, though. Not drowning nor rising from the water. But I *was* here, walking with Christopher over the bridge and getting our feet wet in the lagoon. Then I don't know, he was sprinkling a baby with holy water, baptism obviously. Outside of the fact that I was *here,* I have no idea whether any of that has any significance."

"Hmmn," Ariyah replied. "Nope, I've no idea either, dear. Let's head home."

"Good idea," I said. "I'd like to get back on my regular schedule, though. Perhaps we could stack up the night with activity after we return. You're on spring break now, correct?"

"I *am,*" she returned.

"Excellent," I confirmed. "We might go to an evening church service, then dinner, drinks, dancing, and back home to watch movies the rest of the night."

"Wait a minute there, woman, back it up to the first thing," Ariyah interjected, not sure she heard me right. "A *church* service? You want to go down *that* road again after this morning? Are you nuts?"

"Oh no," I replied, clarifying. "There'll be *no* engaging in *any* Communion, don't you worry! With whatever's happening to me, I would just like to be in God's house tonight, but *if* there's a Lord's Supper served, we're out of there before it ever starts, believe me!"

"Okay," she said. "I guess. I think that one I went to with Joe has another service tonight, but it's Protestant. I liked it, though."

"Perfect," I replied. "Much less likely of taking the sacrament twice in the same day as a Catholic church, all the better. I don't care what 'flavor' we go to."

"It's settled, then," she concluded as we were about halfway home. "We'll book up our night till we drop! Then I'll sleep all day with you. It'll be fun!"

"That's fine," I responded, "to *sleep* together, but nothing *more.* Call me old fashioned, but with you involved with Joe and my bent toward Christopher, I'm *not* looking to be intimate. It wouldn't be right."

"Would you listen to 'Miss Conservative Monogamous Vampiress'?" Ariyah cackled. "Haha, no, we don't need to get it on, m'dear. It's not as though we're some committed gay couple or anything. We've just experimented because we're friends, and what you do for me as a dominatrix kind of spun it off in that direction. No worries, no expectations, love."

"Thank you," I said, squeezing her hand with a wink as we walked on.

CHAPTER 13

Christopher

The cab ride journey to and from Old Town to Woodlawn was beginning to feel familiar now, though I wasn't at all sure how comfortable I was with it. I was a Catholic priest traveling to and fro with an ever-growing involvement with a vampire, for God's sake! Until a few days ago, I didn't think that was even possible. But as a good Christian, I *had* to take responsibility in it; *I* invited it, invited *her.* And now I was in so deep, I allowed her to make sustenance of me.

Don't get me wrong; I *was* coming to believe the Lord was indeed doing a work here; I was feeling it on a supremely spiritual level. But so, too, was I feeling it on an emotional and relational level as well *with* her. And I couldn't know how it would play out and equalize all together, maintaining who and what I am. For one, there would undoubtedly be immediate consequences for my absence to the last Mass I was to conduct.

Secondly, I'd promised to accompany her on a journey to the West Indies to seek out her maker, a vow made in haste, purely out of instinctual loyalty. Or was it *more* than simply loyalty? Was it not the natural attraction of a man to a woman? And was it *not* the ultimate in irony, the paradox of what two souls *could not* have? Not merely a lady and a gentleman but vampire and a priest—what could possibly contrast more? I don't know.

But I soon would *know,* that is, the results to the abandonment of my post this morning past. Upon my exit from the cab and reentry into the parish, my superiors met me with a stern and quick leave of absence. I'd attempted to explain myself with untruths, of course. I could in no way be forthright in the details to a woman *and* a vampire! My muddled story of a "friend in need" clearly did *not* cut it.

So rather than a typical Easter Sunday wind down, I was faced with packing to go elsewhere for a week or two. Beyond the initial shock of the sudden, extreme mandate, I found that I was actually all right with it. It would give me time away to ponder my life with the church and God in comparison to this new relationship with the vampiress. I would contact an officer friend of mine at the USO of Illinois, where I used to serve as chaplin, for a place to hang my hat for a spell. There, however, would be a good distance from here, North Chicago, making that pending rendezvous with Charissa for a run highly unlikely.

As the day wore on into later afternoon, making my call to Frank at the USO and finishing my packing, I fell into a place of respite for a short while. Not quite a nap, merely a rest. During which, I found familiar imagery beginning to creep into my psyche again. Refreshingly, it was nothing greatly disturbing this time. It was Charissa, of course, and myself taking a walk. I assumed she must've been asleep and dreaming at present.

We'd traversed over a moon bridge, thus indicating probably Jackson Park, the Garden of the Phoenix. It appeared there was no intent on her part in that moment of communication, for we did *simply* that—strolled with no conversation. The next sequence showed us moving from the bridge to the bank of the lagoon and she getting her feet wet while I looked on. Disjointed imaginings then followed. First there was her emergence from beneath the water, rising up, clearly reminiscent of her "purging" and vision from earlier in the day. After that, I saw her frantically feeding upon me again, once more from before. As I'd described at the time, she was like an infant milking on a bosom. Lastly, *that* broke into seeing myself sprinkling a baby in baptism.

"Let us draw near with a true heart in full assurance of faith, having our hearts sprinkled *from an evil conscience, and our bodies washed with* pure water."

It was then that my mind refocused and snapped back, echoing those words from the book of Hebrews. Though I'd wanted to move along to things of immediate concern, I still found myself in review of the succession of images. How was it they connected? I felt that somehow, they must. Moving backward to forward, the child being sprinkled, the adult feeding but acting childlike, and the woman rising from the water, it all painted a picture of Charissa's rite of Baptism! A baptism by fire, as it were—fire to ashes and a Phoenix rising there from! To me, it couldn't be clearer. I sensed, though, that it still remained blurred to her. Perhaps sometime soon, I'd be able to share my insight, offering some clarity.

As for now, I awaited the Navy corpsman Frank offered to send over to pick me up. A thoughtful gesture, considering the distance and my short notice. Though this *was* Chicago, I felt the sense of *in a* "New York Minute, (Everything can Change)" I believe Don Henley once sang. In the course of one day, it seemed much had for me.

In a short while, the transition was becoming more complete. It was roughly five thirty, and my ride had arrived out front. I loaded my bags in the back seat and joined my driver in the front. He introduced himself, Corpsman Cliff Brown, as we sped away from the parish.

He shared that the timing of my visit was good, as their chaplain was currently away for a few days. "God works in mysterious ways, eh, Father?" he commented.

"You have no idea," I responded with a chuckle, considering what my world had now become.

As we traveled I-94 to far North Chicago, I relaxed into my seat and rested a bit more. In so doing, I continued to have impressions of Charissa; this uncanny link of ours seemed to be in no danger of being broken. As I had just left a church, I felt the sense of she *and* Ariyah entering one.

Initially I was very wary to this, wondering why she would risk the possible reoccurrence of what we'd already endured this morning. But then I had a more peaceful wave flow over me, feeling that she was simply seeking out a deeper sense of God in His house. Moreover, I felt that she would in no way flirt with the disaster we'd previously experienced.

As such, I deepened my relaxation, entering into a prayerful place, one focused upon Charissa and whatever work it was God might be doing in her. I would remain doing so until our arrival and Cliff stirring me from my reverie.

Charissa

The church service at Urban Village Methodist went well for us, splendidly so, as a matter of fact. The topic was perfect for the evening service following Easter morning: Jesus's interactions with his disciples post resurrection—a natural progression if you ask me. The subject captured me greatly, considering the presumptions we all shared in what seemed to happening to me. It appeared I could be in the process of some kind of resurrection from *my* parasitic life. Thus, how Jesus carried on with those he was close to, in light of *his,* truly captivated me.

For here I was with the support of both Ariyah and Christopher as I navigated this strange path. As I listened, reflected, and drifted in what I was hearing, I thought I felt the impression of Chris *with* me, praying for me. This made me feel peaceful, humbled, and loved.

Ariyah showed her care for me then, too, with the nudge of an elbow to my side, pulling me out of my drift. She eyeballed to the altar area where they were beginning preparations to serve the Lord's Supper. Then she cocked her head toward the exit with urgency.

"Agreed," I whispered in answer, wasting no time getting up for a hasty retreat. We moved like pack animals hurrying to return to their den. There were a few judging glances from people in disdain to the timing of our exit. *Too bad,* I thought; they would never know the favor I was doing, sparing them the very real possibility of *true* blood consumption if I remained.

*****

In a short while, we toasted wine glasses (nonrepresentative of blood) at the restaurant we'd chosen for dinner, the quaint Piccolo

Mondo in Hyde Park. "To the fools who are far too quick to judge based on what little they perceive," I said.

"Salute," agreed Ariyah. "They would've been grateful to get us out of there if they only knew what could've been in store."

"Absolutely," I concurred. "Honestly, honey, it's *those* attitudes within the church, both in the hierarchy and the sheep who follow them, that's contributed to my being away from it for so long. That and the night creature which I am not belonging there."

"You shouldn't say that, Chris," she returned. "Doesn't God love *all* his creatures? Be they of the night or the day?"

"Yes, but that doesn't mean the leaders and the people do. Trust me, when you are a cursed thing, it's *not* a good place to be."

"Well, I don't see you that way. But you feel the 'curse' is being lifted, you think? Is that why you felt okay going tonight?"

"Not so much *because* of the possibility of its release but rather *due* to it. I sought God's workings themselves *in* his house. I wanted to see if I could get intuition to the process itself. As far as 'approved' to be amongst the people, I couldn't have been less interested. They could all be herded into my dungeon to feed on for all I care."

"Woowww," exclaimed Ariyah at the rawness of my honesty. I guess it *was* a little blunt. "And *did* you?" she continued, again playing with her pendant, "get any intuition, that is?"

"Yes, actually. That sermon opened my eyes to some things. For one, there was the fact that Jesus's bloodletting *did* have an end, giving me hope that my feeding upon it might also have one. And two, his resurrection returned him to his humanity and to his people. But at the same time, he was evolving, becoming something more, which would lead to his accession. I feel a parallel to me in this. Don't misunderstand, I'm *not* equating myself to Christ. I'm just relating, getting it, getting *him.*"

"I understand, I get *you.* Anything else?"

"Well, besides that and comprehending the *power* of blood more than ever, I also sensed Christopher praying for me, I think. But he felt distant, as though further away than his parish. I wonder if anything happened?"

"Could've. He *did* leave his Mass to come to you today. That might not have gone over very well with his superiors. You think they sent him away or anything?"

"As I said, church hierarchies can be very intolerant. They certainly could've done something like that. And dammit, that's on me."

"Can't disagree with you there. But hey, water under the bridge. You can't beat yourself up over it, just figure out what to do with it, if there's anything *to* do."

"What to do would be to find out for sure," I said. "If our guesses have any basis, calling the church would be relatively useless. They wouldn't tell us anything truthfully. Would you mind, Ari, if we didn't go dancing immediately after dinner so I could take a nap and see if I can 'find' Christopher?"

"We can skip it altogether if necessary, sweetie. If you need to reach out to Chris and *can,* then do it, absolutely."

"Well, it surely isn't an exact science, this dream communication, but it's been working pretty good so far. So yes, once we finish dinner, let's go back to the apartment and I'll try. No rush, honey, enjoy your food."

"It *is* good. I just love this chicken vesuvio," she said, devouring another bite. Then preparing to wash it down with another sip of wine, she raised her glass again with a "Salute" and a touch to her pendant.

It was good just to relax like this with my friend after the chaos of the day. Though I was growing more curious about what may have happened with Christopher, I found my curiosity was equally mounting over her plaything of a pendant.

Finally, I just asked her outright, "Ari, what of your charm necklace? You've always had good taste in accessories, but I've never noticed one quite as much, what with how much you've been toying with it. It *is* quite beautiful—"

"Oh, this?" she asked, fidgeting with it all the more. "I've had it forever. I got it at a craft market in Nassau as a kid. The blue crystal just mesmerized me, and after I begged enough, my mum got it for me. It's Caribbean I think."

"Hmm," I replied, pondering. I rewound my brain to when I'd first noticed her touching it a lot, and it occurred that it was when I'd been relating the story of my perils in the West Indies, the Caribbean.

"What?" Ariyah blurted after I'd gone silent too long in my musing.

"Oh, I just find it interesting that you say its origins are of the same area that mine as a vampire are, and you began playing with it incessantly when I told the tale today."

"Really? Oh yeah, I did, right! It's so unconscious, I barely realized," she stammered, catching herself from doing it some more. "Wow, that *is* kind of freaky!" Then *she* paused, thinking upon it herself. "Wait a sec, you don't think it's connected somehow, *do* you?" she abruptly exclaimed.

"I think it would be a very long stretch, but we *have* experienced the bizarre and unlikely this day, so who knows?" I concluded. And with that, we dropped the subject and returned to toasting yet another glass of wine.

After our lengthy dinner, we set back out into the night with every intent of walking the entire considerable distance back home. As we strolled the city blocks walking and talking, I began to get the sense of being followed. I felt as though a presence had attached itself to us, maintaining a safe distance but *definitely* keeping pace. It's pretty difficult to track a vampire and remain undetected, our senses being what they are. But this was different; whoever, *whatever,* it was, matched my own sensory abilities. Another vampire? An animal? Time would tell as we continued our path waiting, watching, listening. For the moment, I said nothing to Ariyah.

Then she made a move that pushed everything forward, not realizing. She saw a fashion shop she liked and darted for it. Unfortunately, the shop and those adjacent to it were an inlet row, which dead-ended. Beautiful. I circled around to keep her from going in, but I was too late; I hadn't realized the inlet immediately, and now we were perfectly cornered to our pursuer. Which, at that point, wasted no further time in at last revealing itself.

First, there was one, then two, then three *dogs.* A little pack of street mutts, just starring us down. I cradled Ariyah into me, moving us both backward; the pack, of course, continued to pace our movements. She gasped; they growled. Then something strange happened. As we all inched further into the dead-end behind us, the growls turned to a less-intimidating grumble, they're eyes catching some reflected streetlight. They were *blue.* The blue druzy of Ari's pendant. Naturally, as I turned to her, she was unconsciously clutching it once again. She looked at me, then glanced into their eyes, finally returning her gaze to the pendant, taking in its color as she opened the palm of her hand, showing forth the stunning blue agate.

That was the last moment of respite there would be for the next few minutes. The grumbles returned again to growls—the kind announcing an imminent attack, and so they did. First the lead dog, a heeler, lunged high at us. I pushed Ari aside and ducked under him in one swift movement. Getting under his belly, I reared upward and, using his own momentum, flung him yelping into the inlet's dead-end wall.

The remaining two, a pit and a ridgeback, charged without leaping, learning from their point-dog's folly. I punched the Rhodesian in the jaw, sending it reeling. Still, the pit got me in the shoulder blade but only chomped on it, not locking on. It sought more, wanted my throat before clamping its jaws down tight. Too bad for it as I thrust my mouth forward and got to hers before she got to mine! Biting down, my fangs dug in deep; then I pulled out, ripping away a nice chunk of fur and flesh. She yelped and released me simultaneously, then whimpered away.

Unfortunately, the heeler was back and bearing down on Ariyah. She was caught between her fear and attempting to take action. In so doing, her hand again went over the pendant, completely enfolding it within her fist. Suddenly, I noticed the blue in the dog's eyes that matched the stone began to diminish as the pendant was obscured. And that gave me an idea. I bolted toward Ari, kicking the dog in the face as I reached her. Then I grabbed the pendant by the chain, tore it off her neck, and threw it up to the rooftop above us! At which point, the blue glow of all the dogs' eyes completely returned to a normal color. They all paused momentarily as if coming out of a daze, shook their heads, then turned and trotted away.

Initially, Ariyah was stunned at my brash move of ripping off her necklace; but once she'd seen the result in the dogs and their simultaneous departure, she understood somewhat, though not entirely. "What just happened, Charissa? I mean, I just *saw* what went down, but I don't get it. How do the eyes of a pack of dogs reflect the color of my pendant, and how does it go away from them when you tossed it? Why did they attack us? And how the heck did you learn to fight dogs like that? It was amazing."

"Let's see," I said, running through the series of questions. "I don't know, I don't know, I don't know, and *I don't know!* But my prowess for dealing with canines? Let's just say I've battled wolves before back when I first came to America. As for the other questions though, I may have some ideas. Listen, before we get into that, what say we get out of here and get a taxi home at this point?"

"I should say *so*," she returned, still in shock a little. "We need to get you cleaned up from that bite. Your shoulder's kind of a mess."

"Oh yes, that," I said. "In due course, I'll heal quickly enough. First though, excuse me while I go retrieve your necklace." That said, I bounded up to the first rung of the building's catwalks, quickly scaling the rest of the way up to the roof with my vampire speed.

As I did, Ariyah shouted to me, "Wait, I don't know that I want it back if it's cursed or something!"

Yelling back, I said, "We'll *need* it back if my suspicions are right, Ari!"

To which, a dumbfounded look crossed her face, which maintained until I came back down. "Here you go," I said, attempting to hand it back to her.

"No thank you," she replied, pushing it away. "Much as I *do* love it, I don't want it anywhere near me till we figure out what the deal is with it, sorry. You keep it for now, please. It should stay with the one who's got half a clue. You *do* have a theory then?" she asked as we finally left the inlet, returning curbside to hail a cab.

"I do. I'll tell you about on the way home." And I did once we acquired our ride, Ariyah shielding my bloodied arm from the cabbie's view as we settled in.

"All right," I began, "so you're from the Bahamas, where you got the pendant in the first place. And the Bahamas being in the general region of the Caribbean wherein lies the point of origin of my turning, the West Indies, home of my cannibal shaman maker. I lost track of him, but maybe he *didn't* lose track of me. Maybe he traveled to the Bahamas to a craft market where he could place a talisman into the ownership of one who would eventually meet me."

"Oh come on, Charissa!" Ariyah exclaimed. "That's a helluva stretch! How could he possibly know that, in advance, when I was just a kid, for God's sake!"

"How indeed?" I replied. "Because he *is a shaman* perhaps? A shaman who might have had dreams and insights into the future, maybe? Think about it. I've never given it an inkling before, but look at what's going on with Christopher and I. We're *dreaming* to each other. Could that not be an ability passed on to me from him, my maker? A maker who's *more* than your average vampire? Who has skills of magics? *And* who may have placed some magic into a stone so that it might serve as a kind of homing beacon when activated? Again, think about *when* this thing with the dogs occurred. I'd been talking *this very day* of perhaps seeking him out in *your* presence, *with* the pendant on. And the dogs' coming up on us was his 'calling card' to get our attention."

At that point, Ari bellowed out a monstrous cackle. "Wowww, Chris," she began, stammering through giggles. "*That* is a brilliant piece of work! Did you dream all that up just now, or have you been working on it awhile?"

"Don't make fun of me," I said, "I'm serious. If you've got a better explanation, I'm all ears."

"Absolutely *not,* my friend," she answered. "I couldn't even come close to anything resembling an explanation. You've done that at least. At most, though I hate to admit it, you may actually have something there, far-fetched as it sounds."

"I know it is, honey, but it does make *some* sense, doesn't it? The more you think about it, I mean?"

"Tell you what, Chris, give it a rest for now, and I *will* think on it the rest of the way home. If it seems less crazy by then, I'll let you know. Fair enough?"

"Very well then," I agreed.

CHAPTER 14

Christopher

I'd let Frank take me to a pub nearby the USO to have a couple of beers. This far away from home, and considering the day it had been, it seemed to me the perfect idea. And ironically enough, I believe I sensed an impression of Charissa and Ariyah having just done the same thing, though wine over beer. To which, I found myself shaking my head in more disbelief to all that was happening.

Frank caught this and asked, "What, Father?"

Since I was a priest in a bar, and it is said that bartenders and priests are the best listeners, I decided to confide in Frank and make him *my* server since he was picking up the tab anyway. I told him much, though not all, of my current situation. The supernatural part was left out, of course, as I didn't need him thinking I was losing my mind altogether.

"Ah, ha-hah!" Frank laughed knowingly. "It's always a woman that gets us in the end, eh Chris? Even if you're a padre! That's rich. Pretty shitty though, your cardinals kickin' you out for missin' a Mass. I know you said it was over this Charissa gal, but I thought the church had progressed beyond that crap by now."

"Perhaps in some cases," I replied, "but obviously, not in this one, not this time."

"Guess not," he answered. "Well, there's plenty o' Catholic fathers out there who take wives. I 'spoze ya just gotta find the right parish that'll accept ya bein' a regular man, who naturally, wants a woman!"

I didn't recall at any point telling him I was thinking of marrying Charissa, but perhaps Frank just made the natural progression with where my tale seemed to him to be going. That's fair. As I thought of Charissa again, I was now getting a bad feeling regarding her. Danger perhaps, of some kind to her and Ariyah.

Still not having a direct phone number to contact her and being so far away now, I had to go with the only option at my disposal. "Frank," I said, "I appreciate your ear and the ales, but it's been one long day. I think I'll head back and catch some rest now. I don't want to rush you out of here. If you wanted to stay on—"

"Yeah, you go ahead, Father," he began, his gaze meandering to a redhead drinking alone. "Think I might see about 'a woman getting me in the end…' of the night, if you get my drift. Night, Chris."

Yes, I got his drift. It was the same as mine, hoping to find my woman by the end of the night, if not sooner. Did I just say "my woman"? Good Lord.

When I got back to the USO and into my room, it proved easy enough to reach my desired goal. It had been a long and arduous day, and the beers consumed were just what I'd needed to put me out almost immediately. As I'd laid myself down to rest upon my cot, I put my thoughts into focus, reaching out to Charissa, asking God to connect my dreaming to her. As the saying goes, "Ask and you shall receive."

Soon I found myself not in the bed where I was but in my own back at the parish. I bolted up and out quickly, going for a run, I assumed, toward Charissa's apartment. I knew that neither she nor I were currently in either of these places, but my subconscious, I suspected, was drawing more upon the familiar.

Suddenly, as dreams will do, I found my venue changing. I was still running, still seeking her out, but now I was on the lakefront, and up ahead, I saw her. It struck me that we seemed to be reenacting our previous meeting during a run. I slowed as she turned around to come at me.

"Chris," we both said simultaneously to each other and then embraced.

"You're not anywhere near *here*," she whispered before I could say anything else myself. "Are you?"

"As you aren't either," I reminded, pulling out of our clinch and looking intently at her. That gaze, though unintended, was pulled away as I caught something in my peripheral vision. It was Ariyah running toward us from the same direction Charissa had come. Trailing her were three dogs in hot pursuit. I didn't even have a chance to say, "What in heaven—" before she darted past us trying to escape them. Then no sooner had that happened, Charissa produced Ariyah's pendant and suddenly heaved it out into the lake. The dogs veered off, and Ariyah continued on her merry way as if nothing out of the ordinary had occurred.

I found Charissa's eyes again, giving her a confused look.

"*That*," she began, "was the danger you may have sensed we were in from earlier this evening. It was a little unnerving at first, but once I figured it out, it was nothing serious. And your evening, Padre? *I* have sensed not danger but *distance* now between us, more than there was. I suspect something happened at the parish when you returned?"

"Yes, my superiors didn't take kindly to my absence at the third Mass. I was given a leave of absence for probably a couple of weeks. I'm now up in North Chicago with a serviceman I used to pastor at the USO. He was kind enough to take me in on short notice, and as it turns out, his priest is away, so it's all very equitable. But tell me more of these strange dogs and how Ariyah's pendant being tossed to the lake dissuaded them."

"*That*," she continued, "is a long story, one that took some time to piece together. Suffice to say that I believe the dogs were taken over by some power in the pendant. Did you notice the blue in their eyes as they went by? The same blue as the pendant's gem. My guess is that it originates back to my maker. I believe it's possible that he's been tracking me at a distance since it landed in Ariyah's possession as a child. Us being together and talking about him, speaking of seeking him out, I think activated something in it, causing the dogs to be controlled. When I tossed the pendant away, the influence over the mutts ended."

"I see," I said, hearing but not entirely digesting all she had explained immediately. "So I suspect that this development has you more determined than ever to go after him?"

"Naturally," she replied. "But first and more presently, I'd like to address this growing expanse between *us,* with you practically in Waukegan now."

"It's not *that* far!" I exclaimed.

"Almost," she countered. "Other than in a 'dream run' like this, it's going to be harder for us to connect like we'd been planning. I wish you'd contacted me first instead of opting for somewhere so far removed."

"I still don't have your number," I reminded.

"Oh, of course," she answered. "Still, you might've given a clue when you appeared to me when I slept in the garden."

"I was *conscious* then, just thinking of you, *not* focused dream communication. My decision on where to go to and who to seek out was completely instinctual in the moment. The life I've known versus the couple of days I've known you won out."

"Well, depending on how long the vacancy left by the other clergyman remains, I hope you'll consider returning to Old Town with me as a plan B."

I honestly *hadn't* considered such; the obvious in-appropriateness of it had likely masked it from my mind as an option. I barely knew her, though the intimacy within this blood bond of ours was surely nullifying that fact.

So I said simply, "Of course, I will do that." On an entirely different note, I continued, "Now, something for *you* to consider while I *am* here: Northwestern University in Evanston, about halfway between us. It's a research school, and I know someone on the faculty. Would you think about meeting there to provide a blood sample?"

The pause that ensued told me I'd indeed caught her off guard.

Finally answering, she said, "Excuse me, but for what purpose? I don't understand where this is coming from."

"A place of intrigue and curiosity," I replied. "Since hearing the story of how you came to be, it crossed my mind that there could've been something unique to *you* in all of it. Specifically, if there were a special property to *your* blood which, intermingled with those of the cannibals, caused an effect that would manifest *only* within you."

"Hmmn," she murmured. "Sounds like I'm not the only one who's trying to piece things together with a lot of conjecture. It's not that this has never occurred to me over the centuries. I just never pursed it. But if you want to, I'm game. We can do it when Ariyah and I return to my place in the next couple of days. She wants to go to the dungeon for a session."

"Once again," I began, "your extreme activities are *your* business, so I'll not speak to that. But I'll take your number *this* time so we don't have to continue to rely on dreaming to each other to make plans."

She agreed and gave it to me, which I remembered and noted upon waking up. It was strange; I found it scribbled on my hand like a schoolboy getting a girl's number or making crib notes for class. Apparently I found a pen in my sleep and took it down. I felt that same youthful excitement in at last procuring it, like a lad would when he got her number. It wasn't a big deal really, but it still felt like some kind of milestone in the course of our strange relationship. At least it would finally add some normalcy to it all.

Charissa

I awoke happy that I'd finally given Christopher my number but angry that he was so distant now and angrier still at his superiors for sending him away and angry at myself that it was mostly my fault—*too* much anger to not be dealt with. So I arose and stalked out, marching down my street with purpose and determination. I rounded the corner after several blocks and climbed the stairs to the entryway of the parish. Flinging open the double doors, I blasted inside shouting, "Cardinals! Come and face the wolf you sent your shepherd away for!"

My voice echoed loudly through the stillness of the vacant church, reverberating in ghostly fashion. Then silence. No one dared to come answer my calling. So I went to them, moving fiercely yet stealthily upstairs to their quarters. Conveniently, they were gathered together for what appeared to be a meeting over a meal. Fitting, inasmuch as I was about to make a meal out of them. Out of nowhere,

I produced restraints from my dungeon's assortment of playthings, and suddenly they were all held to their seats for me to pick through like a buffet line.

I hopped up atop the table and strode around, kicking food to the floor. Not all of it though, as I decided to pick up the bread loaf as yet uncut into slices. I palmed it and said, "*This* is your bodies about to be broken for me for taking away my priest so callously. And *this*," I continued, picking up a flask of wine, "is your blood about to be spilled for my sustenance, *your* penance to *me* for Christopher's banishment."

I then shook up the bottle and proceeded to crack it open in a gush of wine spray aimed around the table at all of them. As they shook their heads from the alcohol on their faces, I suddenly held in my hand a longsword. The blade's length allowed me to stride the course of the tabletop walking upright while slicing their necks as I went. They all slouched forward, dying, as I got down from the table and went around it, sampling each of them.

They tasted very good, and though I'd been mad at them and had judged them as misguided, I felt the "God essence" from their blood. I craned my head back in euphoria, taking a satisfying deep breath, waking myself up with a gasp again.

*****

"Hello again, my vampire friend," said Ariyah, sitting next to me on the couch, where I'd apparently nodded off watching television with her, after we'd gotten home. "Was I boring you, or was it the program?"

"Neither," I returned. "Just a dream message from Christopher calling out to me that I must've dozed off to answer." It was more than that, obviously. My nightmare rampage upon the priests was another clear factor of the dream. But at least I didn't feel angry at them anymore. If I *was* undergoing a metamorphosis to bring me to redemption, I clearly had a long way to go. The dream made it apparent how much darkness still resided within me, my taste for vengeance remaining strong.

Ariyah reached over to me and touched my arm. "I'm guessing from that look you just had waking up, there was more to it than just Christopher."

"And what look was that?" I asked.

"The one you have when you're enjoying your work. I've seen it plenty, at least when you don't have me blindfolded." She chuckled. "But never mind that. I'm more interested in what Christopher had to say—"

"Well, we *were* right," I began. "He *has* been sent away, a leave of absence for the missed Mass. He's up near Waukegan now, at the USO, where he used to pastor. His friend there took him in, no questions asked."

"You don't look too happy about that," observed Ariyah.

"Stop watching my 'look'!" I chided. "You're right, though. I *don't* like it one bit. But when you and I go back to Old Town, it looks like I'll be going up to the research university to meet him. He has some notion to analyze my blood and see what makes me tick."

"Well, that's weird," she replied, "but at least he's taking a real interest in you, however nerdy it is."

"I imagine so," I acknowledged, "but who knows? Maybe I'll actually learn something that's useful in relation to the shaman and our connection."

"Do me a favor," Ari continued, "in all the exploration of *connection* to priests and shamans, don't forget about *ours,* please?"

"Never," I replied, leaning my forehead into hers. "I will attend to you and ours as soon as we go back to Old Town and get both our minds off all this for a spell." I gently moved our heads back from each other to look into her eyes, then grinned at her. She smiled back with the corner of her lip curled at me.

I'd been consistent to the subject of our backing off from each other through the course of the day, but in that moment, I couldn't resist kissing those curled lips. We fell into it and canoodled for a time, then I grabbed the TV remote and turned it back on again. "Let's watch another movie and push it till dawn, sleep the day, then get out of here and go back to Old Town. What do you say?"

"I'm all in," she answered, still pleasantly smiling.

CHAPTER 15

Ariyah

It was later the next day, late afternoon approaching dusk, as we taxied back into Old Town. It was Charissa's idea to test herself in the waning daylight again, which seemed to go pretty well. I still wouldn't let her do it without the hoodie on as a backup, just in case. She was quick to ditch it on our arrival to her flat and entrance into the dungeon. She happily tossed it aside as she entered her changing area as I did mine, flinging my own jacket atop hers with a glance and a wink back to her.

I don't know what it's like when she's entertaining male clients, but when it comes to *me,* I'm always provided the classiest of apparel. I think it allows her to transport both of us back into her timeline a little bit, more so than with the men. For us, it's more about becoming women of history, along with the release of inhabitations.

I exited my dressing room with the anticipation of the session relieving all the seriousness and chaos we'd experienced in the last couple of days. I crossed the room, taking position with my arms over my head, pressing my hands against the wall I faced, my back turned to her door. A moment later, I heard her walk in, stepping toward me.

"Hello, my pet," she whispered just behind my ear.

"Hello, mistress," I replied, remaining still, submissive to her, as she wrapped a blindfold over my eyes.

I sighed to the anticipation of what was to come. I thought I heard Charissa sigh as well, but it contained a tone more of sadness than any satisfaction. I heard her heave another sigh, and this time it sounded distinctly distressed. I was confused. I listened as

Charissa drew and exhaled deep breaths but didn't touch me for some moments.

"Put your arms down, pet," she said disparagingly. "Come," she continued, taking one of my hands and leading me back across the room, my confusion growing.

"Lean over," Charissa said, putting her hands under me as I did. Suddenly, she was beneath my stomach and legs, lifting me up, then laying me face down upon a padded table. My arms were now stretched out in front of me flat. Though I tend to enjoy these sessions immensely, I had no idea what was going on. There was the question, too, of whether Charissa was into it all, which I was beginning to doubt, though I didn't know why.

I knew better than to speak up, but with my vibe that she was "off," I couldn't not. "Mistress, is everything all right?"

"*Do not* question me, pet," she tried to say with force but failed to produce, as her voice cracked somewhat as she spoke. This session, as far as I was accustomed to them, wasn't really materializing.

She moved her hands to the back of my knees and pulled me down the table a degree so that my face fit into an opening in it bored out for that purpose. My head now rested comfortably while she moved to the other end and stretched out my arms, loosening and relieving them by her caress. I listened to her breathe in and out, and it was becoming more even, less filled with tension than her outbreaths from before. She sustained her touch upon my arms but began to increase the pressure she rubbed me with. Soon the pressure was growing intense, painful even, but in a good way. She began to move her strokes into my back and shoulders, burrowing her elbows into my muscle tissue. She would find knots, working them out until we both gasped together in their pop and release. It was all painful and beautiful all at once.

I still didn't know what was going on here; the session never having taken shape as I was used to. The fact that I'd already spoken up, as well as the fact I was experiencing comparable pain and pleasure regardless of the changeup seemed to make doing so a moot point. So I went with it as Charissa dug her fingers into my gluts, manipulating the muscle so well I felt it even into my lower back.

Then she went to my legs with full abandon, applying deep force upon my outer thigh. Succumbing to an excruciating combination of pressure and pain, I exhaled audibly. This pleased Charissa, too, I could tell, as she released her breath also, in sync with mine.

At that point she told me to turn over and helped me do so. She moved her hand across my stomach, then moved it down my side, adjacent. She began to poke around there, as if looking for a way in somehow? She told me to relax and take in a deep breath. As I did, her fingers literally *found* their way in! It felt like she was going through organs to find the deeper muscle beneath. I gasped, turning my head from side to side, squirming. She placed her other hand back atop my belly to still me. After a couple more moments, she stopped and did my other side. We were clearly in very new territory at this point, so I simply asked aloud, "*What* was that?"

"One of the most painful little tricks I know," she answered. "But your lower back will feel wonderful for it later. Now hush, my dear, I'm nearly done."

She moved back up to my head, neck, and shoulders, continuing a barrage of strokes and compressions, taking me back and forth from hurting to healing. By now I was utterly submitted to her but in a completely *different* way than what I'd come to expect as her client. We were in a place of peace and healing now, as opposed to the darker place of where we'd always been before. All except for her finishing touch.

She raised my head then, lifting it up by my chin. I felt her breath hovering there just over my neck, heard her inhale as her mouth bore down, biting into it. I closed my eyes, letting myself just be carried away by it. But before I knew it, she retracted, releasing me from her bite. Strangely, she barely took a wine sample's worth, it seemed.

I sensed her head moving back upward from my neck, which proved true as she lightly kissed my forehead, her hand held over my heart. The dominatrix had never really entered the room; *this* was my friend now treating me specially.

"That's our session, m'love," she concluded. "I'll see you in the kitchen when you're ready. B'bye." She brushed her hands across the sides of my face in departure and then exited the chamber.

By the time I'd dressed and returned upstairs, Charissa was already enjoying a coffee drink she'd brewed while I readied. She was seated casually at the kitchen bar sipping her espresso. As I entered, she smiled, nodding at me to grab myself a cup. I did, and as I mixed in cream and sugar, I asked her, "What *was* that down there? I thought we'd come back here for a normal session, but you turned it into some kind of massage-therapy clinic! Not that I'm complaining, mind you."

"I expected you'd question me about it," she began, blowing into her cup. "It's hard to explain, but something came over me where I just couldn't continue doing that kind of punishment to *you.* I think it must have to do with this 'rebirth' that's happening to me. As I was preparing for our normal routine, I kept picturing Christ being beaten, so too other Christian martyrs. Visualizing them like that, I couldn't go on as we're accustomed to."

"That's why your sighs were so strained then!" I exclaimed, finally getting it.

"Yes," she went on, "and the thought of 'disciplining' you just seemed wrong. But I knew you'd be disappointed if we did nothing. Since I knew other methods that employed painful pleasures, I thought I'd try that instead. So how was it?"

"Oh my gosh," I answered. "It was fantastic! Apparently, bondage isn't all you're good at. If you gave it up, you could make a living as a masseuse for sure! Of course, you're going to have a serious problem working blood feeding into that."

"Of that, I'm painfully aware," she returned. "The sole purpose for being a dominant *was* to establish an environment in which to easily feed. Massage sessions would certainly *not* be the proper setting. Obviously, this sudden moral consciousness creates a serious problem for me."

"No doubt. What with all the attention these days to 'inappropriate' behavior of any kind. That would screw you pretty quick! Maybe you could just alternate feeding on me and Christopher to start with. After all, it *was* through feeding on him that your 'goody-goody' path started. He *ought* to be your regular."

"Perhaps. He'd have to be consulted first, but two potential regular donors beat none at all. Either that or go back to being an out-and-out predator again, just attacking people as the need arose."

"Good luck with that," I offered, "getting squeamish from the mere thought of roughing me up a little." That said, we both just looked at each other for a moment, then giggled.

Her sense of dominance must've returned for a moment as she playfully put her fingers to my neck, lightly squeezing, and said, "Silence, my pet."

And we laughed again.

CHAPTER 16

Christopher

I called Charissa on the phone for the very first time, feeling giddy over it, with butterflies almost. It was evening of the next day following that most momentous Easter Sunday. I thought I'd try her in the nighttime, considering the source. I wanted to see if she'd made it back to Old Town yet and, consequently, see if she might soon be available to meet together again.

She was and was still up for my proposal, too, the blood testing at the university. She said she was ready to do the entire venture in the daytime, that she was continuing to flourish in the daylight. I hesitated to the wisdom in this somewhat, but she was resolute that she'd been trying it out thoroughly. I initially suggested that we connect halfway between Northwestern and Old Town at Foster Beach, but she said to make it at Calvary Cemetery since I was coming in from so much farther. Again, I considered the source, the vampire wanting to rendezvous in a graveyard—naturally.

It was around lunchtime the next day when we caught up there, each of us taking taxis the long drive from opposite directions. When I found her, she was under a tree by the largest gravesite, a shrouded-man statue with the headstone written in Latin. She was dressed in running attire, either having already done some of the trip by jog or planning to hit the trail back to the university. A hoodie lay beside her on the ground, sunlight protection I gathered, in case her good luck in the day ran out somehow.

"Hello, my priest," she said, looking up at me with inviting eyes.

"My lady," I answered, sitting down beside her.

"I have a confession," she began, brushing my hair across my forehead and out of my eyes. "I couldn't do it. Couldn't do a full bondage session with Ariyah, you know, like we'd planned upon our return to my place."

"Why's that?" I asked, ever uneasy with this topic.

"Because of you. Because of whatever all this is that's happening to me since I've been feeding on you. We'd just gotten through perhaps a quarter of the session, and I simply couldn't bring myself to punish her. I kept seeing Jesus and martyrs in their tortures, so I just had to stop right then. You want to know what I did after that?"

"What, pray tell?"

"I didn't want to disappoint her, so I turned into a masseuse and massaged the hell out of her! Still equal parts pleasure and pain, and though she was entirely confused, she loved it!"

"That's great," I said with pause, unsure of exactly how to respond.

"Aren't you proud of me? I *thought* you'd be happy to hear of the breakthrough—"

"I *am* happy!" I exclaimed, hugging her, almost a little too quickly, too comfortably. "I just never know how to react when it comes to your 'business.'" We eased out of the hug, facing each other, continuing on.

"I understand," she said. "It's all very taboo to most, especially to one such as yourself, I'm sure. I was never into it by any personal desire to do so. It was ever and always a vehicle by which to incorporate my feeding—a means to an end. If I find that I'm unable to do it across the board with the rest of my clients, I've got a real problem. I'll need an entirely new dietary plan. Ariyah offered herself right away and suggested *you* as well, but I've no idea if you'd be comfortable with that."

I thought about what she said and this time was not as quick to jump immediately "to the rescue" as with the swift hug. I simply spoke my mind honesty as to how I *might* offer any help.

"Charissa," I said, "as you've pointed out, you've fed upon me a couple of times now. And those lines *are* gray, 'for someone such as me' in offering to be a regular 'donor' to you. All I can say right now is that I'll pray on it and see where God leads in all of this."

"Fair enough, Christopher. I could ask for nothing more. Thank you. I must say though, you've got an obvious interest when it comes to the 'blood' aspect of things. Ergo, this plan of yours to test my blood."

"Yes," I answered, "I think it's a worthwhile endeavor, certainly. I mean, it strikes me that, given your story, there *had* to be something special in your blood chemistry for things to have happened the way they did, don't you think?"

"Oh, I would agree, of course, given you've made a clear point to it. Again, I've thought about it in the past, just never followed up and did anything about it. I rarely share my tale with anyone, much less have them take enough interest to propose such a thing. So once more, thank you. When are we scheduled for again?"

"In a couple of hours," I replied. "I didn't want us to have to adhere to too tight a schedule today, with time, distance, and what-not."

"Ever the man of wisdom," she offered, unconsciously caressing my back in acknowledgment. I looked at her intently as she did, then she at me, as my gaze pulled her into awareness of her friendly familiarity with me. Then for the first time, rather than disengage from further touch, her hand glided around from my back to down my arm and finally into my hand. We continued staring eye-to-eye through this while my fingers wrapped over hers.

If the current state of affairs hadn't been what they were—away from my parish, far from my post, banished for now, and spending more time with her—what followed probably wouldn't have happened. But it did. Our gazes remained locked, and our heads kept moving closer together. As we were almost there, she took my cheek in her hand, and I held her by her neck. And there it was, tender, soft, and sweet—a kiss, not a bite. It was as it should be for two such as we, lingering and gingerly exploring each other's lips.

It seemed we explored more than that too. As the warmth of our kiss prolonged, flashes of imagery went through our minds. I envisioned the sacrament slowly taking each element one at a time, then saw Charissa in synchronous succession of biting my flesh and drinking blood from therein. I felt the strength she drew from it—

that which kept her "undead" form animated, the clear parallel of the blood of Christ keeping humans "dead in their sins" alive in his light. That same light and power I could see flowing into her from the times she fed on me. Also I could *feel* the eternal life His blood gives us when we receive it in the same fashion the vampire becomes immortal by the taking of blood for sustenance.

Upon seeing these various things under our closed eyelids through the kiss, we both fluttered our eyes open, looking wide-eyed at one another. We backed out of our smooch slowly in mutual satisfaction and alertness.

"That was everything and *far* more than I'd imagined," she said, amazed and licking her lips. "I saw and felt things beyond just your mouth, Christopher."

"So it wasn't just me," I replied.

"I guess not. It's safe to say I've probably done more kissing than you, and I'm hard-pressed to remember one quite like that. It's like I felt the inner *you* as I tasted the 'outer you.' Oh, and God, too, of course."

"Yes, yes, exactly. I felt the surge of strength *you* get as you feed. I felt the power of Christ boost that strength from when you've drunk from me. Indeed, not like any kiss I've ever had either. I think it even makes me feel even a little less guilty for doing it."

"Of course I understand why *you* would say that, *priest,* but if we should continue down this road, and *I* would certainly entertain it, you're going to have get around that, sir. I'll not have myself become a source of conflict that you do battle with yourself over repeatedly."

"As you said, fair enough," I replied. "There is more than enough turmoil brewed up between the both of us presently, without adding to it. So what say we move it along up to Northwestern now then?"

"All right," she said, getting up first. Once I'd risen as well, she touched me on the arm and kissed me on the cheek.

"Thank you for a very memorable kiss, Christopher. Regardless of where we go from here, I enjoyed it very much."

"You're welcome," I said smiling back at her. "Despite my reservations, I did too."

"Now how about a little run up the lake to get that blood of mine pumping?" she asked, starting off into a trot.

Charissa

The path to the university by foot would be a daunting task for many. But we, being the joggers we are, made pretty good time of it. Still, we pretty much ate up what was left on the clock before the appointment.

We took Sheridan Road north out of the cemetery until Clark Square Park, where we diverted to Edgemere, running through about a half dozen beach parks along the way. Finally we came to the Campus Drive after clearing Centennial Park. But we weren't there yet; we first had to cross campus, passing the School of Music, the Museum of Art, the Concert Hall, and the Central Utility Plant, which had a beautiful view of the Lakefill inlet.

But we weren't here for beauty but blood, my blood, and it was pumping high from our run when we finally came to the U-shaped building that was the Chemistry of Life Processes Institute. From what I understood about this place, I felt highly honored to be seen there.

Apparently the focus here is diagnostics of cancer, cardiovascular and kidney disease, as well as infectious diseases, neurodegenerative diseases, and trauma. But more than that, the researchers aren't just clinicians but chemists, engineers and physicists according to what Christopher explained to me on the jog. Quite a place. I understand that Northwestern, by nature, is a research institution, but my word!

Regardless, Chris then rang his friend, and soon a Dr. Cosima met us in the lobby of the Silverman building. She was introduced as a professor of medicine and assistant professor of biochemistry. Impressive.

"Delighted," I said, shaking her hand, feeling her pulse in it. Ever a hard habit for a vampire to break.

"Likewise," she said smiling, though eyeing me quirkily. This one's no dummy. She sensed exactly what I was doing. Either that, or

Chris didn't tell her I was a woman, just like he didn't let me know the same of her. Surprise!

"Shall we?" she asked, arm outstretched, ushering us out of the lobby and to whatever lab room we were headed. As we walked, Christopher blushed, knowing he'd neglected pertinent information about ourselves to each other.

We entered the High Throughput Analysis Lab, and Cosima quickly got down to business—feeling for my vein, securing the tourniquet, readying the needle and syringe.

I reached out to Christopher for his hand with mine, the arm that wasn't getting drawn from. He looked surprised; was I actually grasping for him because I was squeamish to this? In a word, yes. He took it but smirked so much that he nearly laughed aloud. I realized the hilarity of it, a vampire with an aversion to having her blood taken—the supreme of paradoxical punch lines.

"Aww, that's cute," Cosima said, inserting the needle, pulling open the syringe and drawing out the sample. "You should've warned me she wasn't too comfortable with this, Father."

"*I* didn't know," he replied. "I would have *never* guessed she was." He looked at me again, agape. I stuck my tongue out at him in response, then winced some more while the needle remained in me.

At last to my relief, she withdrew. Serves me right I suppose, to know what it's like when I'm biting someone. Of course, I prefer to think I make it more pleasurable than the damn needle. She swiftly gave me a cotton ball to hold over the puncture, then wound tape over it and around my arm.

"Excuse me, you two," I began, "I think I'd like to go visit the ladies' room about now, if that's all right."

"Of course," Cosima returned, "it's just down the hall and to the left. You're fine, I'm just going to start analyzing the sample. Take your time."

"Thank you," I said, turning to exit the lab while Christopher looked at me curiously. I suppose he still couldn't get over the vampire being scared of a needle. As such, I needed a break and had to get out of there. I eventually did get to the bathroom but not before I wandered the hall for a while. I questioned myself for even doing this, but once I caught a glimpse of sunshine through the window, all my anxiety slipped away as I admired the light I've so long been deprived of.

I imagine I must have been fairly basking in it when he came to me, for Christopher was very unnerved to find me so. Apparently, I'd exceeded my allotted bathroom break time, so he came looking for me.

"I don't know why you're out here flirting with the sun, so please, why don't you come away from there?" he said.

I nodded and then finally went to the ladies' room, doing business and freshening up.

In a moment, I'd returned into the hallway with Christopher and walked with him, heading back toward the lab. I took his hand, and he accepted it with no qualms. He suggested that we proceed onward to look for a bite to eat and give Cosima more processing time. I told him to go ahead, but that I still wanted to look in on her. He said he'd wait outside so as not to lose each other in this place. What a gentleman.

I stepped inside once more and asked, "Doctor?"

"Yes, yes," she replied with anxiousness in her voice, waving me over. "I'm glad you're back. I've some questions I'm curious about."

Approaching her, I said, "Certainly, what can I answer for you?"

"Well, funny thing, your blood. I can't really pinpoint a specific type. It's all over the map. Nonetheless, the most consistent type-match I get anywhere near is Caribbean. Or at least close to the ballpark of what you tend to find in that region. You don't appear as though native to that area. If anything, you strike me as perhaps British. What can you tell me?"

This is exactly why I'd always refrained from doing something like this—questions I cannot feasibly answer. *You can't narrow down my blood type, Doctor, because I'm a vampire, and I've all sorts of peoples' blood running through me.* It is interesting though, that she'd detected the derivative of my maker's strain. She's good, I'll give her that.

Finally I just said, "Well, I've had transfusions before," unable to think of another answer.

"Oh, okay," answered Cosima. "I assume that at least one of them occurred in the West Indies neighborhood somewhere?"

"That's correct," I replied with hesitation, growing more frustrated with where this was headed.

"Look, I usually don't do this in blood analysis," she continued, "but can I swab inside your mouth to get a DNA sample? I'm beginning to think I'm going to need a little more than blood to get to the bottom of this."

"Of course," I answered with even more pause. But in that moment, as she went for the swab to approach my mouth, I determined to end the charade, having grown weary of it. Before she got there, I played a little distraction, taking her wrist and admiring her bracelet. But I didn't stop there. While I had her wrist, I brought it closer to me, deeply inhaling her scent, wetting my appetite. I then released it, having clearly weirded her out in the process.

"Now, Doctor," I said, "watch my *teeth* closely as you swab please."

She nodded, hesitating but acknowledging, and gladly taking her hand back from me. As she got into my mouth and swabbed, she observed my canines protrude in all their sharpened glory.

"Oh my god!" Cosima exclaimed, drawing back quickly. "What the hell! Stay back, you…you…"

"*Vampire* is the word you waver to say, but you now know to be true," I proclaimed. "Don't worry, I'm not going to bite you. I just took in your scent like that to get them to come out. I imagined seeing would help you believe. Your questions were mounting, and being less than forthright at this point can only be a waste of time to both of us."

"Well, thank you, I think," she returned, still steadily wary of me. "That would certainly explain the multiple blood markers in you and why pinpointing a singular blood type would be next to impossible."

"Exactly," I concurred. "You're obviously good at what you do, and since Christopher blocked out time with you, I could no longer see the point of more pretense. Speaking of Chris, he's waiting for me outside to go get some food while you work. May I rejoin him, or do you need me further?"

“I think I’d like to keep you around if I may, so go send him on the food run and pick up something for me, too, if you would.”

“Perfect,” I said. “Are you sure you’re all right with this now that I’ve spilled the beans?”

“I don’t know, Charissa,” she replied. “I’ve never met a real-life vampire before.”

“That’s how Christopher felt a couple of days ago, dearie, and as you can see, he’s now quite fond of me.”

“Well, I wouldn’t expect the same of me, but I think I’m okay with you as long as you keep your fangs to yourself, and get me that snack.”

“Yes, ma’am, done and done,” I answered, scurrying out of the lab and hustling back to my priest. *My priest.* There I go again. Who did I just say was fond of whom?

CHAPTER 17

Christopher

I'd been waiting for her longer than I would've expected by the time she'd reappeared, sidling up to me somewhat friskily. "What took so long?" I asked.

"She was having difficulty," Charissa began, "can you imagine? Trying to narrow down a vampire's blood type! Sooo I helped her out with it."

"You didn't," I stammered.

"I *did!* Showed her, actually. She wanted to swab me for DNA to help out the process, so while she was in my mouth, I extruded my fangs, then told her about it."

"I'm sure that went over really well," I commented.

"Better than you might expect, actually. After the initial shock, it all made a lot more sense to her. You probably didn't want me to say anything, but it was bothering me that she's so diligent to make a determination while I withhold the most pertinent information of all. I mean, she's quite the professional, so I felt I just had to."

"I can't fault your logic whatsoever," I replied, "but I cannot believe you came out with it!"

"Believe it *or not!*" Charissa joked. "And believe *this,* too. She's hungry and wants you to get her a snack. She wants to keep me, so you're on your own, sir, sorry."

"See what happens when you bring out the fangs, Chris?" I offered. "You make others around you hungry too!"

She laughed in agreement as I rose to go make the food run. She got up as well, giving me a surprise peck *on the lips.* I suspect as a thank you for doing it?

"You're welcome," I said, "but I haven't gotten any food yet."

"You oaf," she began, "not *just* for getting us food but for setting this all up and bringing me here, for allowing me to feed on you, and simply for the fact that I like you!"

"Oh, well, okay then," I replied, half stuttering, still not really sure what to do with this budding relationship. She giggled as I turned to make my way and find the cafeteria. Glancing back, I observed her continuing to do so as she went to return to the lab. To this, for whatever reason, I grinned as well.

As I looked about to locate a campus directory, my phone rang—an incoming call from Frank at the USO. *I wonder what this could be about,* I thought. He began clearing it up right away as I happened upon the guide map I was looking for.

"I hate to do this to ya, pal," he began, "but our padre's getting back tomorrow. I thought he was gonna be away longer. Now, I can look into what we can do ta get'cha another room but no guarantees. I'm sorry, Fadda."

"Don't be," I replied, "and no problem if you don't have anywhere else to put me. Charissa had been disappointed that I hadn't let her know of my staying with you, had wanted me to stay with her in the first place, I believe."

"Aw, well there ya go, my man! You are one smooth priest, buddy. See? I'm tellin' ya, you gots ta find a parish where they're cool with married ministers, man. So I'll expect ya later to clear out then?"

"Okay, Frank, I'll come by with 'the missus' in a couple of hours so you can meet. I'm with her now. We're getting something to eat."

"Ha, of course ya are! All right, man. I'm glad to see yer makin' the most of yer time away from the parish. Good job. I'll see ya later."

Well, it looked like Charissa was going to get her wish after all with this latest development. As I found the cafeteria and placed an order, I mused further over "development." That of hers and my relationship, that is, how it's been escalating, even *this* very day. Kisses and handholds. What shall it be under the same roof? I shuddered to think the temptations of the flesh. She'd be upset, but perhaps I should stay with Ariyah instead. Or better yet, *she* could stay on with Charissa, and I could remain at Ari's by myself. It would be a distance, but one we're accustomed to, not the vast chasm of the USO to Old Town. Even as I thought it, I knew she'd balk though, say I'm overthinking it and complicating things. Regardless, my order came up ready and stopped me from analyzing it further. Good. Nothing more to be accomplished by delving further in my own mind versus simply talking to her and resolution through open communication. That's what we fathers counsel the married folks on anyway.

With my food order in hand, I made my way back to the lab to find Charissa and Cosima thoroughly chatting it up, reviewing test results. They both seemed ecstatic, with any possible apprehension on Cosima's part to Charissa's vampirism fallen by the wayside.

"Father," Cosima began, plowing into the bag for her Asian chicken salad. "I'm glad you're back. Your friend here is quite the enigma! Had she not fessed up to her 'condition,' I fear we'd have made little progress. But in *knowing*, we've now made great strides! By taking the DNA sample, I was able to narrow down her likeliest *original* blood type, Rh negative.

"Now, though *not* uncommon, it *is* the most mysterious. No one's been able to explain where people with the Rh negative blood type came from. Most admit that these people must be the result of a random mutation, if not descendants of a different ancestor. There's evidence suggesting the Rh-negative blood group may have appeared about 35,000 years ago, the Basque people of Spain and France having the highest percentage of Rh negative blood. Their language is unlike any other European language. Now, *you'll* love this, Father. Some believe that Basque was the original language of the book of Genesis. Some even believe it was the original language of the world and possibly of the Creator."

"That is phenomenal," I said, the wheels in my mind churning wildly.

"Not only that," Charissa interjected, "it makes perfect sense, as my father was French! I'll leave the divine implications for you to ascertain, my priest."

How courteous of her to saddle me with interpreting of the grand design of it all.

"Moreover," Cosima continued between bites, "in certain instances, blood groups common in people of Northern European origin can make for suitable recipients to transfusions from Afro-Caribbean donors. Which, in Charissa's case, sounds like exactly what may have happened after a fashion. I cannot account, of course, for whatever supernatural factor the vampirism contributed, as that is well beyond the realm of my expertise."

"Of course," I reiterated. "As far as *that* is concerned, we can only rely upon Charissa's lengthy know-how in *living* as one for so long."

"And just how long is that?" Cosima asked.

"A couple of centuries," answered Charissa.

"Are…are you kidding me?" countered Cosima. She looked upon Charissa's straight face and saw that she wasn't. "So I suppose, Father, that she kind of *gets* those folks who supposedly lived so long in Genesis?"

Charissa

I suppose I sort of did, now that she mentioned it. I'd never thought about it that way before, but with what was happening to me lately, it was kind of hard not to. I know I *just* said I'd leave the "divine interpretations" to Christopher, but Cosima's take on Genesis possibly being written in Basque originally, *and* maybe even being God's own language; well, I suddenly couldn't stop thinking I'm on some kind of chosen path now and had *been* on it for longer than I could've imagined—a path that was somehow leading me back to my "immortal" maker designed by my *true* maker!

The ramifications were about to make my head explode when Christopher at last broke me out of my ever-growing reverie.

"I expect she *would,* yes," he said. "A sobering revelation indeed," he continued, placing his arm around my neck and shoulders, soothing me. He'd clearly grown to sense when I was overwhelmed, which helped immensely in bringing me back around.

"It seems this endeavor has been productive to say the least," he went on, "so may I offer my thanks to your seeing us today. I think, though, that Charissa has all the information she needs now. If there's nothing further, I might ask that we excuse ourselves?"

"Absolutely, Father," replied Cosima. "You're more than welcome to stay and finish your lunch here with me."

She looked in the bag again to see what might have been there for me and, in seeing nothing, said, "I could look in the fridge and see if there's any blood I could spare?"

"That would be thoughtful," I answered, "thank you."

As she went to see what she could find, Christopher apologized and said, "I didn't know what actual food to get you. Please forgive me."

"No worries," I answered, "but for the record, other food I *do* eat is meat, of course. You know, part vampire, part cannibal. Not that I'd give into that, but animal flesh is close enough, beyond blood."

"Noted," he replied.

After she'd returned with a little something for me and finished our lunches, we bed Cosima a fond farewell, thanking her once more for her hospitality and all her efforts on my behalf. She walked us back out onto the campus, where we took leave of her.

*****

Upon returning to the surface streets, we hailed for another cab, whereupon Christopher informed me of our next destination. I was both surprised and delighted that his stay at the USO was coming to a close. As we traversed northward to the Waukegan area, he was forthright as to his reservations in staying with me. Although this failed to equal my initial pleasure to this turn of events, I did appreciate his honesty, and understood. Nonetheless, I did find his concerns to be, well, a tad prudish, but that's me.

He shared his thoughts as to the possibility of trading places with Ariyah, and I agreed that it could work, at least for the short term. I reminded him that she'd need to go back the following week, upon the conclusion of spring break and her return to school. *And* that naturally, we'd need to confer to see if it was amenable with her in the first place. I would find out soon enough: we would never have *that* conversation.

*****

In the meantime, our arrival to the USO and meeting Frank was all pleasant enough. From his grins and approving looks, I could tell that Mr. Frank would *not* be one who'd share Christopher's hesitations in cohabitating with me. And if I weren't wrestling with how I felt about it, I'd entertain having *him* in my dungeon.

Despite all his concerns, I *did* pick up from Christopher's demeanor that he'd taken some manly pride in introducing me and showing me off a bit, which lifted my hopes for us in a positive direction just a tad.

Prior to our gathering Christopher's things, Frank informed us that he'd have a man drive us back to Old Town, as had apparently been done for Chris when he first came here. As such, Frank insisted on taking it leisurely and hosting us at the nearby pub for some ales. Good man, Frank, here's to you.

Christopher wasn't a lot of help, but we'd consumed one pitcher and were halfway through a second when I dismissed myself from the table. I wanted to go call Ariyah and let her know we'd be back in a while. Drat, no answer. Perhaps she was off seeing Joe or something. I'd try her back in a bit.

Since I was already in the rear of the establishment, I decided it was time for this lady to freshen up once again. As I finished my business, I proceeded to wash up. After splashing my face, I glanced into the mirror; and following seeing my own image, I mysteriously thought I saw Ariyah *with the pendant on* and something shadowy behind her. Foolishly but instinctually, I spun around to check behind me, and naturally, there was no one there. When I turned back to the mirror again, it was just me—no further odd visions. I blinked to be sure, then turned to wipe my face. Just to satisfy, I looked a final time at nothing more out of the ordinary.

I returned to the table to join my boys, but what I'd seen in that mirror had dampened my spirit of revelry somewhat. I strained a smile; poured myself another glass; and took a good, long swig. Nice try, but I couldn't get the reflection of Ariyah out of my mind. What could the shadow behind her possibly have been? And why did she have the pendant back on? Sure, I'd left it behind, but she'd not taken it back from me either. Wait a minute, the pendant, its color, wasn't its normal blue; it was red. Bloodred! All our talk of it being activated, it's a blood beacon! The pendant back upon her, the shadow behind, it's my maker coming to take her, to draw me out! At this realization, I slammed my glass to the table, now totally commanding the attention of the men, whose curiosity to my mood change was already on the rise.

"What is it?" asked Christopher, more than a little concerned.

I looked to Frank first apologetically, "Please excuse me, Frank, I'm sorry, but," then turning to Christopher, I continued, "We have to get out of here *now!* I-I had a premonition in the ladies' room. I think Ariyah's in trouble back home."

"Did you call her already?" he queried, asking the obvious.

"Of course," I replied calmly, pulling out my phone once more. "But I told myself I'd attempt again, and no time like the present." I held up my index finger to signal him I was trying, as he and Frank murmured between themselves.

"No dice," I concluded, ending the call. "Straight to voicemail. We should go, Chris." He nodded to me in affirmation, then again to Frank in apology.

Frank then dashed up to the bar to pay the tab, but I sidled in around him, slipping my bank card over the bill. "I've got this," I said. "It's my fault for us having to rush out of here. Please, let me."

He started to argue, but I had my best dominatrix demeanor going, so he let it go and allowed me. Since I'd bumped him on that, he redirected himself to something else, getting on his phone and talking to someone named Cliff. He asked him to get a jump on getting Christopher's things together and driving us back to Old Town. I appreciated his initiative in rallying a hurry-up in response to my state of panic. We simultaneously finished the payment and phone call, thus making haste out of there. I touched his arm and told him thank you for his foresight.

"No problem, Charissa," Frank replied. "When something's up, we servicemen hop to it, y'know. What *is* up anyway, if I may ask?"

Christopher and I both looked at each other to his question and answered in unison, "It's complicated."

CHAPTER 18

Christopher

In the time we'd scurried from the pub to the USO, we did give Frank at least *some* explanation to his question. Charissa was forthright to her concerns over Ariyah's safety. The larger, supernatural side to the picture she kept to herself but would share with me once we were on our way.

But we had to get back to the USO first. Once we did, Cliff was there with my things packed and loaded in a car. One thing I have to say about Frank is that he's money in a crisis. Whatever needs doing, he's on top of it, and Cliff too.

Charissa thanked Frank once again, this time giving him a hug. She was grateful to Cliff as well, but in just meeting him, she only shook his hand. I both shook hands and hugged Frank goodbye.

"Gotta winner with this gal I'd say, Padre," he offered in a whisper before we broke away. "Now go take care of her friend and keep me posted, will ya?"

"Will do, Frank," I answered. "Thanks for everything."

Once on our way, in the privacy of the back seat, Charissa backgrounded me on what happened in the pub's bathroom.

"As I was washing up, I glanced to the mirror, saw myself, of course, but then Ariyah's reflection. She had the pendant on, and it was *bloodred.* Behind her was a shadowy silhouette shrouding itself around her. Separately, the elements didn't make much sense, but once I put it all together, I concluded that I probably don't need to go seeking out my maker. I think he's likely come to us, by way of the talisman-pendant, and it's with *her!* Since she's not picking up, I'm afraid he may have taken her or something."

"Or something," I replied. "She could've just gone out to see Joe perhaps?"

"Of course I thought of that. But why wouldn't she pick up? For me? I'm sorry, but I'm not prone to whimsical imaginings. I believe I saw what I saw *for a reason.* No, we're doing the right thing hustling back now."

"I suppose you're right," I answered. "So, you associate that 'shadow' with your maker, do you?"

"I *suppose* if you're fishing for holes in my story, a simple shadow might mean nothing. However, the *last* thing I saw was the bottom of the shadow trickling *into* the pendant, from around her back, up to her chest and the gemstone. That, in my mind, is the catalyst connecting the specter to him and so on to her."

"Because you've already established that the pendant originated from your maker, it seems to me there's a fine line between establishment and conjecture."

"Yes, yes, Christopher. All my deductions thus far could not be admissible as anything but circumstantial evidence in a court of law. Granted. I don't even care that you may doubt my theory, but when it comes to my friend's safety, I'm not taking any chances, whether my ideas are a stretch or not."

"Of course, I agree, better safe than sorry."

"Absolutely, Christopher. Just as you've pointed out recently, *we've* only known each other for a couple days. Ariyah I've known a couple of years. We all gravitate to the familiar first and seek to protect it. Just as you would your flock."

"A fair point," I concluded. We both fell silent then, with little more to say. She'd shared her intuitions while I'd countered with my doubts. She wasn't angry with me nor had I become skeptical of her. We'd simply spoken our thoughts and they weren't completely in line with each other. So for the rest of the ride, we simply held hands and prayed for Ariyah. Cliff glanced at us in his rearview occasionally, and though I couldn't see his face, I knew he was smiling approvingly to our closeness.

While dropping us off at Charissa's flat, he smiled again but more strained this time as he knew we were returning in crisis mode to a situation as yet unknown. Charissa only said a quick "thanks, bye" to him as she bolted inside to check things out posthaste. I lingered to unload and bid Cliff a proper farewell.

Charissa

It wasn't my style to just drive and dash like that without a proper goodbye to our man Cliff. But I'd been crawling out of my skin the last hour to finally get here. Although the adrenaline release from running out of the car and up the steps was good, the apprehension to what I would find, or wouldn't find, was still killing me. I practically broke down the door once I tore the key through the lock.

"Ariyah!" I shouted once inside. "Are you here, honey?" I knew almost immediately that she wasn't. I smelled her, yes, but not as though she was present. It was only the lingering odor of one who *had* been but was no longer. I cursed aloud, winced, then dropped to my knees in despair. I squeezed my eyes tight, producing tears. When I opened them again while still kneeling, they caught something lying on the hallway floor, which I could see from the foyer where I'd kneeled. The pendant. Even at a distance, I could see that its color was like that of the mirror vision—red.

As I rose and steadily walked toward it, my mind rewound through the last few hours. Seeing the object already this color in the reflected apparition made me think of what I was doing just before *that,* giving and analyzing my blood. Blood. Blood, stone. Blood, beacon. If that's what this thing *was*, what it'd become. Maybe *that's* what it needs—to tell me more. My blood. I swooped it up and stood there looking at it, standing in the hallway right outside the bathroom, which of course featured a mirror. My mind spun with ideas even more.

I turned and shouted out for Christopher, for I was sure he must be inside by now. In fact, I smelled him entering, which was one of my ideas—his smell.

"Charissa?" he asked, dropping his bags in the living room. "Is Ariyah here, did you find—"

"No, no she's not, but never mind. Just come here. I want to try something, and you're going to help. If it works like I'm hoping, you might just see what I saw, and I'll see it again, even clearer. Give me your hand, Chris."

He approached me slowly, confused at what it was I was going on about. Right now though, I had little patience for slow. I grabbed him, pulled him to me, held him at his wrist, and brought it up to my nose, breathing in his scent deeply. He resisted somewhat, not knowing what I was up to, but that would come clear in the next few moments. Once I'd inhaled him sufficiently, my fangs popped out, and I gave my own self a bite.

As I held the pendant in one hand, I asked Christopher to take the other wrist I'd just bitten into and squeeze it over the gemstone. He still moved with slow hesitation. Ahh, my prudish priest!

"Who's squeamish to a little blood now, Father?" I giggled as blood slopped over the pendant resting in my palm. Having plenty on it now, I pulled my wrist back from him and walked with the necklace over to the bathroom mirror. I held the pendant in a claw grip and flicked the blood upon it across the glass, along with a good amount of excess blood from my wrist. Then I gently rested the necklace down on the vanity in front of the mirror. I backed away, bumping into Christopher who was behind me, staring in utter confusion at me and my strange little ritual.

I laid my right hand over his, tapping it and said, "Just wait for it, Christopher."

I glanced again at the gemstone, and its red color seemed to be fluxing, like the oozing of a lava lamp. Then I looked back at the mirror. At first I thought it was my imagination, but after staring at it closely, I was seeing wisps of the same color fluidity in the gem within the mirror.

What I saw next confirmed this course of action entirely. It was definitely *me* in the mirror, but the "me" I was at the time of my turning. There I was lying dead apparently, in the Caribs village, almost entirely drained of blood. I averted my gaze for a moment as this wasn't a pleasant memory, moreover, one I've tried my best to forget.

When I looked back again, my lifeless self still appeared but so did Darvisch, the shaman, approaching me from behind. I've done my very best to erase him from my mind over time, but seeing him like this in the reflective surface brought his damnable name back to me. Even in discussing him over the past couple of days, I'd still not allowed his given name to enter my thoughts. But there it was; there *he* was in all his vampiric, cannibalistic glory bewitching me, biting me, saving me, *turning me.*

After a few moments, I couldn't even watch anymore, I just closed my eyes. Unfortunately, this may have been a mistake. In no longer viewing it, I *felt* it—his breath on me, my teeth in his wrist taking in *his* blood—the little bit *I* had left comingling with his, all of it funneling together, recreating me as a monster like himself.

So intense was the feeling I had to turn around to see if he actually *was* behind me as the mirror's imagery suggested.

And there we stood face-to-face; his, a macabrely painted visage starring me down, mine with the pained expression of reliving a nightmare. He stretched out his arms before me, as if in pride of his conception—myself. Then he placed his hands upon my shoulders, running them down my arms, gleaming his wicked smile in satisfaction.

He leaned his head in closer to mine, his foul breath disgusting, and whispered in broken English, "Look, pet, to the mirror." He turned me around to face it once more.

Pet, I thought, the same word I would use to Ariyah when dominating her. Frightening, the parallel. And then yet another. What he was having me take note of in the mirror image *was* Ari at the marketplace as a child, at *his* booth, purchasing the pendant and apparently some earrings as well. Oh my god, my deductions had been spot-on!

I saw a flash-forward series of visions of her, speeding through her youth into a young woman, all of them with her gemstone and earrings on. Finally, there was she and I together, meeting and becoming friends. And the pendant glowed as he appeared ethereally behind *her,* grinning. It was all true; she'd been chosen as his herald unto me, utterly unbeknownst to her. A pawn to keep tabs upon his true *pet.*

And now this, *the reveal.* In showing me, was he calling to me? Though I'd just seen him again in the glass, I also still felt his perceived presence behind me standing there, placing his hands around my waist. I closed my eyes in simultaneous revulsion and revelation, inhaling and exhaling heavily in the clarity of the moment. Then I turned back around to him and opened my eyes.

I stood back into reality as it was no longer Darvisch but Christopher facing me. My legs physically gave out to the whole experience, but Chris held me up and steadied me. I latched onto his forearms, woozy.

"Are you okay?" he asked.

I didn't answer, I didn't care if I was or not; I just wanted to know if he'd shared the vision.

"Did you get all that, Christopher? Did you see?" I asked with anxiousness.

"I did. Hard to believe the vividness of it all. It almost reminds me of the goings-on I experienced during an exorcism I once assisted on. Based on what we just saw, I guess I can't call your theories conjecture anymore. What prompted you to use your blood on the gem, and what made you think it would work?"

"Honestly, just the progression of what I've been learning about the pendant. What our 'conjecture' already was, plus what happened today, the blood work, then the premonition at the pub. I simply put it all together, and my intuition said to try it. Did I know it would work? No, but my instincts said it might."

"And within what we saw, have your *instincts* derived the whereabouts of Ariyah out of it all?" asked Christopher.

"Well, it *does* seem pretty clear to me from the last mirror image. Darvisch behind her while she's wearing the pendant. He's taken her, then left the gem behind for us to find. Since it's my determination that it's a beacon, I'll use it as a locator to home in on them."

"In the Caribbean, yes?" Chris queried. "Do you think he actually came all the way from there to kidnap her and lure you back?"

"*Get* her and *lure* me, yes. Whether he's physically come all the way to Chicago, I don't know. The incident with the dogs speaks to me of an ability to manipulate things from a distance. He could have relayed by a spell to someone already here to get her, or he could've possessed Ariyah herself somehow, brainwashing her to leave town and go to him. We could find out easily enough, track her banking and see if she's purchased a flight. I *am* a service provider to her. She's charged a session more than once. Easy-peasy."

"You can't just log into her bank account, can you?" asked Christopher, probably wondering how deep my dastardly deeds go. The answer was deep enough!

"All I have to do is figure out username and guess a password, and I'm betting I know her well enough to take a few good stabs at it." So I pulled out my laptop and got down to business. I already knew she was Citibank, as I'd said. Christopher hovered about as I began. That is until his phone rang, and he politely dismissed himself to take it. I nodded and continued my bit of detective work.

Naturally, my success wasn't immediate, but eventually, I hit the right word combinations, and the system started logging me in. Just about then, my phone rang too. It was Joe of all people.

"Hi, Charissa, it's Joe. I'm calling for Ariyah. She'd wanted me to let you know that she's left for a family emergency back home in the Bahamas. I drove her to O'Hare earlier this afternoon, and she went out on a flight to Miami."

As he was saying, I'd scrolled far enough to see the charge for the flight.

"And you hadn't thought to call me sooner than this?" I asked, perturbed.

"Sorry, I *just* got back a little while ago, hadda bite to eat and I'm calling you *now,*" he finished, giving me back some tone himself.

"No, *I'm* sorry," I replied. "You didn't know any better. Tell me, Joe, was she acting strangely at all?"

"Well, now that you mention it, she *was* a little distant, like not quite all there, I guess. I figured if it was a family crisis, maybe she was just stressed about it. Do you think it's more than that? Something else?"

"Possibly, I don't know for sure. I'm checking on a few things now. Do you mind if I call you back when I figure it out?"

"Yeah, sure, I'd appreciate that. I hope you're wrong and it turns out to be nuthin' beyond what she said."

"Me, too, Joe, me too," I replied, hanging up, all the while knowing that sadly, I wasn't wrong. It was "family" business, yes, but not the natural one Joe presumed, rather, her extended, *super*natural family.

CHAPTER 19

Christopher

I'd wandered down the hallway, milling about as I took my phone call. It was from the parish. Unexpectedly, the bishop informed me that it had been decided to bring an early halt to my suspension; that in hindsight, it had been deemed extreme to keep me banished for a full two weeks. He said I could return at any time and to be prepared for next Sunday. Having caught me entirely off guard, I simply acknowledged the news and thanked him for the reinstatement.

I don't think I really meant it though, for when I hung up, I just stood there in front of a door I imagined might be the stairwell to the infamous dungeon. It wasn't truly gratitude I was feeling, for I'd let go the burden of my responsibilities and was more entrenched unto the concerns surrounding Charissa and now Ariyah.

I returned to join her just as she was concluding a phone call herself.

"You'll never guess," she began, "who *that* was! Just as I found a flight charge for Chicago to Miami to Nassau, Joe calls to tell me that *he'd* delivered her to the airport himself! I guess it's the brainwashing theory that holds then."

I heard her but was still processing the news from *my* call. And she could see it.

"Christopher? You okay? Who called *you?* You look like you've seen a ghost. Or one of my mirror visions!"

I didn't really want to say because it would open a whole new can of worms, which wouldn't help our current situation one bit. But the cat was out of the bag as my face's expression had betrayed me. And she'd easily sniff out anything that wasn't the truth.

So I came out with it. "That was the bishop at the parish. He called to inform me that my suspension has been lifted, and my duties shall resume in preparation for next Sunday."

The pause of silence was deafening. Now her face echoed the same blank stare as my own.

"So Joe," I began quickly, desperately trying to rally us back to the situation at hand, "took her to the airport and sent her off. Do you think a spell was cast by Darvisch from afar to make him do so? You spoke of that as one possibility—"

"What?" she snapped, blinking, as though she was elsewhere (I *knew* where*)*, and coming back to the question posed. "Uh…yes, that's *possible* but unlikely I think. He sounded clear of mind about the whole thing, confused to her abrupt behavior and departure. I believe he merely met her need for the lift and that the Darvisch influence was singularly and entirely upon *her.*"

She sighed deeply then and rose from the desk and her computer, facing me sternly.

"Christopher," she began, looking at me intensely, "when I spoke to Joe, he asked if I thought there was something more going on than just a sudden family emergency. I told him I wasn't sure but that I was working on it and would call him back to let him know. Now you tell me, when I make that return call, do I need to ask *him* for accompaniment when I book *my* flight to the Caribbean? Are *you* still with me in this, or are you returning to the parish and your life now?"

This was all happening too fast—Ariyah's being taken/motivated to leave for Charissa's maker so far away and this sudden mandate for me to return to my duties, my calling. I didn't know what to say. I fumbled, literally, fumbled the ball.

"Charissa, I…I…" I babbled.

"Very well then, Christopher," she said. "I can see you're torn, that's fine. But for where I'm going, what I'm *doing,* I require companions who are resolute. Perhaps Joe will be that companion, and I'll ask him if he's up for it, when I call him back. But after all you and I have been through these last few days, what I *thought* we were coming to be to each other, I'd become entirely comfortable that *you were that* companion. It seems I may have been mistaken."

"No, no, you weren't," I began, finally getting some semblance of communication back. "Not entirely. It's just a lot to sort out as you said, 'everything we've been through,' what's going on with Ariyah, your maker, your transformation, and yes, my life, my calling. It's all come crashing together all at once, and I simply need to seek out God on what to do. If you can't grant me that—"

"Not mine to *grant,* Christopher. You've got to figure it out for yourself. So go to God and pray. Go back to the parish and seek sanctuary and your path. Just don't take too long because my time is short. It would mean a lot to me if you were with me, but if you aren't, I'll understand. I think for now, you should probably go. Come, I'll walk you out."

Once again, a *New York Minute* had come to Chicago, changing everything. She walked me to the door, my bags in tow, *leaving,* when I'd finally come here to stay, at least for a night. Why did all of this have to happen at once? It is said that God doesn't give a person more than they can handle, but right now, I wasn't handling it.

She leaned into me, saddened, I could tell. I wasn't very happy at the moment either, so I hugged her back for comfort.

She looked up at me then and said, "I'll likely be in touch with Joe tonight, perhaps even go see him to explain things. I doubt he'll be open to the strangeness of it all nor willing to go with if I just tell him over the phone, perhaps not even then. Beyond that and making flight reservations, I'll not be long in remaining here. If I don't hear from you, I'll leave a message as to when I made the flight for and you can let me know what you've decided, all right?"

With great pause, I at last replied, "Very well." Turning to leave then, we both took a long final look at each other. It reminded me of when we'd first caught glances at the park Communion when she'd jogged by. But those looks were filled with newness, curiosity, even apprehension; but this was just painful. I truly hoped this wouldn't be the last time we'd gaze upon one another, but if I failed to go with her in the end, would she ever *want* to see me again? She said she'd understand, but would she really?

I could even feel her melancholy stare piercing me as I walked away and into the early evening. If I'd been her client beyond the door I'd passed inside, I'm sure she'd have unleashed a good dose of "discipline" upon me about then.

Charissa

I'd called and arranged, somewhat regrettably, to meet with Joe around eight o'clock. I say with regret because up until the moment of that cursed call from the bishop, I'd had every intention of making my long journey *with* Christopher. Why wouldn't I have? But now, nothing was certain. What would Chris finally decide? What would Joe think of it all? I had to be prepared, ultimately, to go it alone if I had to.

I fully intended to go all the way to him by cab or even meet up in the middle, but Joe was kind enough to offer to come my way and pick a lady up. Once here, we were off and found a place to dine and talk locally, the Old Town Social Sports Pub. After arriving and being seated, we ordered some drinks and appetizers, then commenced the conversation.

With him, I wasn't really sure where to begin, so I opened with his point of reference in all of this, Ariyah. I started with when she and I met, then backed up to his familiarity of her being from the Bahamas. From there, I rewound to her as a girl there and buying the pendant. After that, I went no-holds-barred into the pendant's seller Darvisch, what he was, what he made me, so on and so forth. For the third time that day, I pulled someone's wrist up to my nose, his, bringing out my fangs, proving the vampirism. Finally, I offered that her trip wasn't likely a true family emergency but a brainwashed ruse to call *me* out and how I planned to acquiesce.

I let all the information just simmer with him for some moments prior to asking him if he'd consider coming with me. Before I had a chance though, he started asking about Christopher, as he'd met him together with me, and I'd said nothing of Chris up to that point, obviously still feeling freshly wounded over him.

Then came *the* question: "Isn't the Father going with you?" Joe asked.

It is rare that emotions get the better of me; hell, rare that *anything* gets to me really. But Joe zeroed right in on my raw wound, and for the second time tonight, I winced tears out of my eyes.

"Joe," I sniffled, "I don't know. That day you'd met Christopher and I, he'd come to my aid, as you know. He'd been suspended from his church for doing so because he'd missed his last service on account of it. Well, his superiors called him back tonight, lifting the suspension. Now he's struggling with what to do, go with me on this trip or remain here and return to his duties. Though I fear he's already made up his mind."

"So you want me to go with you instead, is that it?"

"It's up to you, Joe," I said. "I'd prefer accompaniment on this journey, and I can't think of a better person, someone Ariyah cares about, you. But *I'm going*, for her, with or without anyone else. And I'm leaving as soon as I can as there is little time to waste. So please, pardon my abruptness, but you're either in or you're not."

"Yeah," he began, "that *is* a little abrupt. I dunno if my answer would be different even if you *weren't* putting me on the spot. Don't get me wrong, I wanna help Ari if she's really in trouble, but honestly, all this shaman, cannibal, vampire stuff is a little over the top for me, lady. No way I've got a clue about any of that. Don't think I'd be much help to ya in all of it. Seems to me like your priest'd be better with that kinda thing. Maybe he's done some exorcisms or sumpthin'. So I'm gonna have ta say pass. I'm good for gettin' ya over to O'Hare though."

Unbelievable. Zero for two in the stretch of an hour and a half. When did men become so wishy-washy? But what could I do? Compel him obviously, but that would wear off eventually, and it's a long trip. Reupping my control over his will would become redundant, and I wasn't going to go there. I didn't need a zombie; I needed someone *with* me.

So I replied simply, "Thanks, Joe, that'll be helpful."

"Sorry, Charissa, it's just way over my head. I'd rather be straight with you up front than go with and just end up being useless."

"No, you're right for being honest with me. Listen, since you offered to take me to the airport, do you mind sticking around while I find a flight after you take me back home?"

"Sure thing."

CHAPTER 20

Joe

I'd waited at Charissa's while she got busy to find a flight out. Even let me check out the place, including her dungeon. Wow. She and Ari were certainly into some kinky shit. Kinda cool, though. Wouldn't mind participatin' in some o' that.

Anyway, she'd managed to find a red-eye for the early morning *this* same night, whaddya know. So before you knew it, we were on our back way to O'Hare. Never expected I was gonna make myself a little career as a shuttle driver to and fro to the airport. We'd yakked just a little on the way, but nuthin' major. She was kinda distant. Probably pissed that both her prospects for travel companions went bust. I didn't blame her.

The thing was, that from the moment I dropped Charissa off at the terminal, *I* started blaming *myself.* I'd tried to pass it off, had asked her if she was gonna call Father Chris back and double-check with him on what he was gonna do. She'd said yeah, but I really didn't believe her. I think she'd given up on him. But on my drive back, racking my brain over not stepping up to help Ari, *I* decided *not* to give up on the padre, not yet.

I got home beat up from a loonngg day but didn't exactly get straight to sleep. I'd doze off a bit but kept waking up, thinking about Father Chris. Charissa and Ari, too, but mostly him 'cause me and him were the ones who'd stayed behind like little cowardly rats. I mean, I'd meant what I'd said to Charissa that this was all out of my league, but that still didn't make me feel any better about it.

I'm not one to go to church much; Easter Sunday with Ariyah was one of my couple times a year. But I'd decided pretty much a couple minutes after I woke up that I hadda go see Father Chris today and talk about all this.

Christopher

The entire night had passed, and morning had come *without* hearing from Charissa whatsoever. Of course, I'd not contacted her either, and that had been laid out as one of our options. But I hadn't come to any decision as yet, so my calling her would've been pointless.

I awoke and strolled around the church and the courtyard in prayerful contemplation. What was I to do in all of this? I walked about for a while quieting myself so that when I finally knelt down to pray, my mind wasn't racing with thoughts. I was tranquil and open to receive. But though I was attentive and waiting, no answers or ideas came, at least during my quiet time there outside with God.

When I returned inside, however, that was a different story. There, within the pews of the sanctuary, sat a familiar presence.

"Joe?" I asked, going to him and putting a hand upon his shoulder.

"Yeah, it's me," he said, looking up at me.

"What brings you here?" I asked, surprised, expecting he might have likely been with Charissa.

"Guilt, I guess," he answered as I sat down next to him. "I should've gone with her, man. She just wanted company, but I was all like, 'it's outta my league. 'I wouldn't be much help.' Blah, blah. Fact is, I just plain woosed out on her and Ari."

Is *that* what I'd done too? "Woosed out?" I'd convinced myself I was in a crisis of faith versus relationship, but was I really? Had I perhaps just gotten scared when the rubber met the road?

"Well," I replied, "If guilt is your dilemma, Joe, you've come to the right place. We offer absolution to the chains of guilt and shame here, and you've basically made your confession"

"What about you, Father?" he came back. "You're here and not with her either. And I know that you know that *you* were her first choice anyway, not me. I was just a plan B."

"So she's gone then?" I questioned. "I never heard from her confirming."

"Yep, outta here. Took her to O'Hare early this morning, and I haven't stopped thinking about it since. That's why I hadda come to you, straightaway today. I couldn't think of a better person to talk to, confess to than the other guy who's bailed on them too. You got any advice, Padre?"

I turned aside from him then with nothing, let alone "advice." Everything he was grappling with, I was too. Since I didn't have my answer yet, I could hardly offer him anything. But maybe I *did* have my answer, that is. In the form of his being here and seeking me out. Perhaps this young man, seeking my wisdom in this equally-shared experience was the very catalyst to bring me to the *right* decision.

"Joe," I began, "my only advice is that you and I set our misgivings and fears aside, pack our bags, leave my church and your school, and get going to Miami and, ultimately, the Caribbean."

"Now we're talkin'," he answered with a renewed conviction. But then, "That was awfully quick, Father. You and Charissa both made it sound like you were gonna muddle over this for a while. What made you?"

"*You* did. Showing up just when I was praying for my answer. You, a young man in my same shoes asking what to do. You've thrust the true answer to the forward, causing me to come to it liken to a first, snap response. Thank you, Joe."

"Uh, yeah, glad I could help."

"We probably shouldn't waste time," I advised. "You said you took her this morning? By the time we find a flight, she'll have nearly a day's jump on us *if* we're lucky. Not our best advantage to catch up."

"Guess that's *our* fault for not makin' the right call to begin with, huh," he said.

I nodded in agreement. I took the reins and rallied us to make haste. I simultaneously searched flights and prepared a letter to my superiors as to my choice *not* to return to duty just yet. I knew this could cost me my reappointment entirely, but the path was finally clear to me now. There would be other positions in the future, but I was sure I would never meet another vampire with whom I'd play as significant a role in aid to their transformation from darkness to light. Hopefully, my salary would cover the pricy airfare before they cut me off. Finding availability on this short notice wasn't cheap. And I certainly didn't expect a college student to have the funds to cover his on-the-fly.

And so, it was done. I packed belongings quickly, and shortly we were off to Joe's so he could do the same. Joe had come to feel that shuttle driving to and from the airport had become his calling, so he took care of our transportation back to O'Hare. After dropping his car off at extended-stay parking, we engaged to the ordeals of security check and flight-and-baggage check-in. By the time it was all said and done, we were right on time for our 1:00 p.m. flight to Miami.

CHAPTER 21

Ariyah

I had no idea what I was doing here. I was somehow back home in Nassau! How did I even get here? I vaguely recalled being in a car with Joe, then on a plane maybe? Had I been in Miami too? I suddenly had a flash of memory of being at Wilcox Field. That would make sense if I'd come home, Chicago to Miami to the Bahamas was definitely the route I would've had to take, but I don't really remember doing any of it.

But here I was, strolling around the old neighborhood, making my way, apparently, to my mom's house. Had I called her to say I was coming? Was I just supposed to go knock at the door, not even knowing, and say, "Hey, Mum, missed you, thought I'd pop in for a visit!" My god, this made no sense.

I had to stop and sit for a minute, try to figure this out before doing anything else, even seeing my mother; and God knows I could use my mom holding me right now. That thought stuck in my mind, being held. Who was the last person who might have held me close? Probably Charissa. Once I thought of her, some things started to click. I suddenly remembered talking to her about the Shaman myths we grew up with here in the Bahamas. Then her whole theory about the pendant *coming* from *her* shaman-maker guy.

Upon thinking of it, I instinctively reached for the necklace, but it wasn't there. Of course not, I'd refused wanting it back. But it had still *been* at Charissa's back in Old Town. Suddenly, I felt the earrings tingling my ears. Jewelry also from *him.* So his little totems that still dangled upon my lobes were giving me a "vibe" when I was figuring it out right. And maybe the one left behind that Charissa *should* have, would be the beacon for her to come and find me? I felt the earrings tingling then again as if telling me, *Correct.*

Okay. If *that* was right, then maybe both talisman, the earrings and the pendant combined, had somehow hypnotized me to, what, fly across the country to go *to* the damn shaman? Why? To lure Charissa, like she'd thought! I knew she'd come for me, but I wasn't in any danger that I could tell, wasn't his captive or anything *yet.*

*****

I blinked for what I thought was a moment then realized it had been longer than that. Another earring tingle told me that was true. Another blackout. Now I was standing at the marketplace. Yes, *the* marketplace. I strolled about like I had my neighborhood before. This recollection brought another memory flash of having been at my mom's front door, knocking quickly then bolting? Why would I do that? Now I'm here, where I'd rather *not* be, as opposed to home where I'd prefer. Obviously, that must've been my own will trying to escape this compelling but not quite getting it done.

I turned a corner of one aisle of booths to go to the next, and then I saw it, *his.* But it was empty. The jewelry, trinkets, and native knickknacks were all there but no one manning the table. In light of that, I took a closer look at the stuff, eyeballing everything to make sure I was on-track to my hunch, then realizing I totally was when I felt a presence behind me swooping over me. *He* cradled me from my rear as I'd begun to black out again, my ears tingling like a fire alarm. He didn't need to worry about being seen accosting a girl; I didn't collapse, just went vacant once more. He didn't *have* to make any moves to my person; I was simply his, like some kind of zombie dog. Just before I was gone again though, I had this sudden sense that Charissa had seen this specific event, yet I knew not how. At least I went unconscious with a good thought because it eased my fading brain that I had the hope of her coming for me.

Charissa

I'd done as much online research as I could on the planes before at last arriving in Nassau. It was to be the final bridge leg of this long journey that would end in the Caribbean. I'd needed to study Ariyah much closer than I ever had before. Yes, I knew about her childhood being here and all I'd pieced together about Darvisch's role with selling her the pendant as a girl. But where she actually *lived* and *where* that damn marketplace was, I hadn't a clue. It took a lot of searching her social media pages and mapping out Nassau to figure out the plan for my next step now that I was here. I was glad for the extensive investigation, though; it managed to take my mind off Christopher and Joe bailing out on me. Those damn fools! Well, so much for that, they were back in my head again. Not for long, however, as my next move was to the marketplace.

I thought about going to Ari's mother's first but thought to make that only a plan B, if it proved necessary. If I found out what I needed here to begin with, I deemed that better than unnecessarily upsetting her over it. Yet as it so happened, it would all converge together at once.

At the start, I used the pendant beacon to lead me to an empty spot in one of the market rows. Not only was the gem gleaming a brilliant crimson red, it was actually vibrating. I knew he, they'd *both* been here. Closing my eyes, I even saw some imagery of the two of them packing up *together!* I'd thought, *Why would she be helping him?* But then reminded myself that she probably was under his spell.

I asked the proprietor of the adjoining space when or to where Darvisch had left. He said it hadn't been that long ago and happened pretty quickly. And to make things more interesting, he went on about how an older lady had come by in a fright, having seen them driving away apparently, as she'd reached the space. He concluded by telling me he thought she might still be at the market's security booth where she'd gone to in a panic just awhile ago.

I thanked him and made my way there. *An older lady,* I thought. Ariyah's mum perhaps? But how would she know her daughter was even *here,* let alone to have an inkling to come to the marketplace?

Unless Ari had the space of a reverie from the hypnosis to try and reach out to home. Maybe she got there or something and tried but got pulled back under the spell and was whisked away again. And *maybe* her mom got wind of her or spotted her as she was prompted back to Darvisch *here.*

Good grief, I was becoming a good little detective! Perhaps it could be my new vocation if I had to give up the bondage gig. Maybe I could dine on bad guys! First things first though, I had to find *my* bad guy. And that, it seemed, was a security booth away. It, however, was an enclosed space—private, non-open air as were the rest of them, as security should be. Not ideal for eavesdropping but hardly a problem for one with vampire hearing. I crouched against the modular building and took a listen.

"I tell you again, I come here looking for my daughter! She come to my door and knock, then leave!" the lady shouted.

"From Chicago?" a man asked.

"Yes, she lives in Chicago!" she answered emphatically.

"So she knocked and left before you could get to the door, and by the time you *did* get a glimpse, she was at a good distance," a second man stated. "So the likelihood of your caller being your daughter from Chicago seems like a stretch. But you followed her to find out for sure."

"Yes, like I've already told you," she replied.

"But you never were able to catch up to her close enough to get a good look before you saw her drive away with a man from the market."

"I don't move so good no more, no. I couldn't catch up to get close. But I know it was her! She went to the old man who sold us the necklace I bought for her as a child."

"The Caribbean guy, right?" the first man repeated. "She went to him, and they packed up and left for the day before you could get there. That makes no sense."

"But that is what happened! I got to the market, to the space he's had for years, and all gone as I arrive! Then I see him driving off in the distance *with my* girl!"

"With *a* girl, you mean," said the second schmuck again. "How many times must I say this, ma'am? You saw *everything* from far off! You can't be sure, and as you say, he's been a solid consignor here for years! He's never been a problem, and you're accusing him of basically kidnapping your daughter who's in Chicago, let me remind you."

I'd heard enough; it was time to intervene. This was going to have to go like clockwork for it to be effective and avoid any violence. I was going to need to be swift and calculated.

I gently rapped upon the door, then entered, and timid as a mouse, said, "Excuse me?" I looked at all three of them to get their full attention, especially the lady. Once I had her eye-to-eye, I continued, "Momma?" With our gazes fixed, I compelled her that this was so. I went to her as she slowly got up, then she hugged me fiercely.

"Ariyah!" she exclaimed.

I turned to the security clowns who had done more hassling than helping and said, "Pardon, gentlemen, I overheard you all and wanted to get in here to let you know I'm fine, no kidnapping. I *did* help the man pack up after I bought something, but that's all. And, yes, it *is* possible for a Chicagoan to show up here in the Bahamas, by the way."

With that, I ushered Mother out and down the steps of the security booth. That had gone perfectly. Now I needed to take back the deception from her and reveal who I actually was because she still had the capacity to help me *truly* find Ariyah, but I needed her real wits about her.

"Momma," I began, gazing again into her eyes, "look at me. I'm not really your daughter. I'm sorry, but I *am* her good friend, and I'm here to find her, retrieve her. I'm Charissa. Can you show me which way they went? *I* believe your story wholeheartedly."

"Alyssa," she replied, hugging me again. "Follow me, if you don't mind an old lady's pace."

"Of course not," I said and just pretended we were moving at vampire speed in slow motion. As such, there was time for conversation as we went. Beyond thanking me for coming, a rapid-fire barrage of questions came: Was I her girlfriend, how did I arrive so timely, and of course, *how* did I make her think I *was* Ari at first? *Not* such an old woman; I would say she was still pretty sharp.

The answers—*kind of* her girlfriend, timely *coincidence,* and whoa, making her think I was Ari? I tried a terrible fib of simply being good at *hypnosis* because I was a psychotherapist? Quite the jump from being an MT. I wouldn't have expected anyone to buy that, but I wasn't about to get into vampires, priests, shamans, cannibals, or cursed objects. Well, perhaps that last part. She had familiarity with the pendant at least, she'd bought it. Maybe I could build some kind of fabrication around that which would be palatable. So much for my godly transformation, concocting a web of lies. But I hardly had time for the long real version, and I didn't think she'd handle that well anyway.

Before long, we'd made our way to the docks of a marina. I took out the pendant from my pocket as we approached. "Recognize this?" I asked her.

Alyssa gasped and questioned, "Why is it that color?" noticing it wasn't blue anymore. "And why do *you* have it? It's Ariyah's."

"I have it because she doesn't want to wear it anymore. As you can see, it's not right, isn't supposed to be red like this. And it's acting strangely. We came down here together to find the man who sold it to you, to see if he could fix it or take it back. Ari went to the marketplace to take care of it but forgot the pendant, only brought the earrings. She called me when she realized she'd left it, and I came in trail with it to complete the errand." There, that all sounded fairly reasonable.

"Why didn't she wait for you then?" she wondered. "Why did she leave with him, and why did she come knock at my door and then run off?"

And there you go, all the holes in my story. "I can't speak to any of that, I'm sorry," I replied. "I told you strange things were happening with regards to the jewelry. Perhaps those odd occurrences are yet another example." Once again, a plausible answer.

She harrumphed and half-heartedly nodded as we walked along the piers to the farthest point out. Looked like I'd finally gotten it right, my pseudo-storyline. Yay. Now it was time to just *look* as far out as I could see. As I was scanning for them, I realized for the first time since my arrival, I'd been navigating about *in broad daylight,* with no cloak of any kind and was doing fine! I hoped my sudden awareness to it didn't screw me and I'd start suffering ill effects because I was now conscious of it.

I put it out of my mind as I located a distant vessel extremely far out. It was so far away that human vision couldn't even spot it, but I could. Once more, I needed a believable explanation to seeing what Alyssa could not, so I placed the gemstone to my forehead between my eyes.

"What are you doing?" she asked.

"Trying out a hunch," I returned. "As I've said, it's been acting peculiar. Perhaps it might give me sight farther than the eye can see?" As I trudged through this latest deception, I couldn't help but think back to when I was with Christopher, trying out my blood upon the pendant. He had been similarly curious as to what I was doing, the same as Alyssa was now. It made me smile. Next I thought of what followed that, which made me frown. My frown enhanced when I heard my phone chirp. Who could possibly be calling me now? Ironically, the caller ID revealed the one whom I'd just been thinking of—Father Chris.

I gestured a pardon to Alyssa and frantically answered, "Hello? Christopher? Hello!"

"Char, hell, I com-ng on m-ay!" he said in a choppy transmission.

"Chris, what are you saying? You're breaking up, where are you?"

"N-pl-n-tr-ng-to-ge-o-yo!"

"I don't understand, Christopher!" I shouted, trying to command clarity out of the damn device, which didn't work. "Hello? Hello!" The call dropped.

"Who was it?" Alyssa pressed.

"Help possibly. It's my priest, my friend. I don't know what he's calling for, whether he's still in Chicago or on a plane to here. Both places could account for the horrible reception," I answered, not knowing which one was a dilemma, but in any case, I needed to commandeer a boat somehow to get out there.

Alyssa had helped me as much as she could in so far as locating Ariyah; now I determined she would be my help in navigating Christopher to me, if indeed he *was* coming. Too many uncertainties, but regardless, I turned to her and asked, "Do you have a phone, dear? Landline, cell, it doesn't matter. And can I have your address here, please? *If* my friend comes, I want to send him to you so you can direct him to me."

"You are going out there after her?" she questioned.

"Well, I'm sure as hell not leaving it to those security fools," I answered with conviction and a laugh. And then she chuckled with me. "I need to get going and procure a boat, but as soon as I'm underway, I'll text the priest, and hopefully that'll get a message through. I'll give him your number and address for if he arrives."

"That's fine, here you go," she said, writing it all down for me. "But how will you get a boat?"

"Come on," I made you think I was your daughter, dear. Do you think I can't work my feminine wiles on one of these boatmen?"

CHAPTER 22

Christopher

I'd waited as long as I could, I thought, to try and contact Charissa. Though the lengthy flights were filled with plenty of time for productive introspection and decent conversation with Joe, once we'd changed planes from Miami to Nassau, I simply couldn't wait anymore. It turned out that I was premature, as the call was broken and eventually dropped. Still I'd gotten through. She may not have known my exact whereabouts, whether we were *actually* on our way to her or not, but at least she now knew I hadn't forgotten about her.

I could hear in her tone that there was a strong will to want to talk to me anyway, a good sign in my mind.

"What did she say?" Joe asked with about the same urgency as Charissa's hellos.

"She couldn't hear me," I returned sadly. "I called too soon I fear. The call was unclear, and she couldn't make out what I was trying to say."

"Forget about calling, man, just text her!" he said, chiding me for being so old-fashioned.

A good point, so I did, explaining that we *were* indeed on our way, though once we approached arrival in Nassau, we were at a loss as to how next to proceed. Some time passed before there came a reply, just about when we were deplaning after landing. Charissa's return text timing was exquisite, with the needed information pointing us to Ariyah's mother; her number and address—perfect.

That all sounded fine, but I was concerned with the fact that she'd indicated she had gotten a boat and was heading out to chase

Ariyah and the shaman down. Regardless of now having a contact, I was wholly uncertain as to how we would catch up.

Charissa

As I'd told Alyssa, chartering a boat wasn't a problem. Between my good looks and my ability to compel, I got someone with a trawler and was upon the sea in hot pursuit of Ariyah and Darvisch in no time flat. Being "hot" though *was* getting to be the problem. Hot, in terms of daylight. Being out in it for so long now *had* finally caught up with me. Curse the luck for thinking about it consciously, all the while I'd been fine until it had actually occurred to me. Now I was feeling overheated, weak, and nauseous.

Worse still, I realized I was also losing strength for not having fed for a long while. The fact that I finally knew Christopher *and* Joe were en route to me was helpful, but they would never reach me for me to feed on Chris in time. Not to mention the fact that I needed to stay topside on the boat to keep scanning for my duo. If I went below for shelter from the sun, I wouldn't be able to keep tracking very well.

Thus I had to opt for a compromise telling the captain I needed to join him in the cockpit. I let him know I wouldn't interfere; just keep a lookout from inside there. Since he was still under the control of my prompts, he didn't have an issue. And as long as I had a clear line of sight upon those we pursued, he wouldn't. I could still see them, too, and that was good. I just had to try and keep myself together long enough, lest I succumb to lack of nourishment, no small task. Between himself and his first mate, the only other aboard, I feared I hadn't a lot of time before I'd give in to the bloodlust.

So another forty-five minutes or so passed, and I'd been self-managing fairly well. I hadn't lost Ari and Darvisch yet, but physically, I was really starting to fade. Because I had him compelled, the captain paid no mind to me. The mate, however, I'd not influenced in any way, and when he came in to confer with the captain, everything went to hell. Before he spoke to his chief, he first noticed me and saw that I wasn't looking too good.

As he leaned to me and asked, "Ma'am, are you okay?" He touched me on the shoulder, and that was all it took. Making contact with me, I felt his pulse, and could imagine the blood coursing throughout his body. And I needed it coursing through mine. Suddenly, I was back where I started when all of this first began staring into a man's eyes, such as with Christopher on the church steps, making him compliant to accept my bite. But today I wasn't toying around snacking upon a wrist, no; I sunk my fangs deep into his neck and drank him in like an alcoholic in recovery who just fell off the wagon.

Thinking of Christopher in that moment probably kept me from drinking him dry and killing him. The metaphor of the recovering alcoholic *was* truly accurate. Christopher was in essence, my "sponsor," and what would he think if he saw me now? If he had stayed on the fence and still remained in Chicago, the thought of him would have angered me, likely causing me to drain the mate to the last drop and finish him. But as I'd learned, that *wasn't* the case; Chris *was* coming after me and *that* made all the difference. In the final analysis, he'd put *me* over the church; and if he could do that, then I could surely stop short of murder. Hell, that's always been the whole point of being the dominatrix—to create the perfect environment to feed without killing.

As it was, though, I *had* rendered the gentleman unconscious by this point. As I released my mouth from him, he went limp and would have fallen had I not held him up. I looked back to the captain to reassert my control of him so that this bloody display didn't produce an undue reaction and complications.

I had already produced one problem by my untimely feeding in the interval I'd taken to have a meal. I feared I may well have lost sight of Ari and Darvisch out there in the distance. I returned looking out to sea and failed to spot them immediately. I decided to tell the captain I was going to brave going topside again.

As I dismissed myself to do so, I had to first haul the mate out of there and take him below deck. I didn't want to leave him there unconscious with the captain. Should Cap snap out of my spell for some reason, I didn't need him wondering what happened to his first mate. I'd wanted to use my blood to heal his neck bite, but after the bonding this had caused with me and Christopher before, I couldn't risk creating another. So I tried a little of my saliva instead, a poor substitute to be sure, but it was something.

I frantically found his quarters, quickly laid him down, took his ball cap for some head protection outside, and bolted back up to the top of the boat. Though I felt rejuvenated, I decided it was time to quit being stupid, not protecting myself from the sun in any way. A cap wasn't much, but it was better than nothing.

And nothing was all I was getting as I stared out across the waves. Even my highly enhanced vision couldn't manage to relocate them, not without help anyway. As I'd attempted previously with it, I pulled out the pendant and decided to try yet another little experiment. First I held it tight and thought hard of Ariyah. With this focus solid in my mind, I held it out upon its chain, praying it might produce more of its magic and perhaps extend outward in their direction? It was worth a shot.

When it *did* perform as I'd hoped, I felt like the witch I once knew having successfully cast a locator spell! I then strained my eyes to their very limits and at last pinpointed them once more, no small feat. Before returning to the cockpit to update the captain, I picked out a cloud formation in about their spot as a landmark. I didn't want to lose them for a second time once I'd repositioned myself again.

As I was about to move, something quite strange happened with *that* cloud. It began to dip downward *toward* their boat like a funnel tail forming! It continued descending upon them, and I gasped in great fear for Ari. I continued in a hard stare looking at where they'd *been* because in the very next instant, they were just gone. There was no debris to be seen that I could tell, nor did I view any splintering of their craft within the funnel as it had passed down on them. Then as suddenly as it had come, it'd begun to ascend up into the sky again. Stranger still, it didn't return entirely back into the cloud where it had been; it just hung there static like a beacon, teasing me.

At that point, in both fright and confusion, I accidentally dropped the pendant I'd still clutched in my hand to the deck where it continued to display its magic. Much like a moment ago, acting as a directional finder, the chain moved itself into a shape a *triangle.* I immediately felt pure clarity, realizing that we'd been navigating all this while within the Bermuda Triangle.

CHAPTER 23

Ariyah

Well, here I was coming to again, this time in a sudden jolt. I found myself in an old sailboat, which felt like it had just jarred back into a normal floating position after being in turbulence. First I looked to see the man I'd felt behind me when I'd last blacked out, in front of me now. After I shuddered to that, I looked about all around me and saw that we were moving over some giant ocean hole in the middle of a larger sea. I shuddered again, wondering if how I thought I'd felt our ship resettle in the water meant we'd somehow just come *through* this hole. Couldn't be, could it?

As if in answer to the silent questions spinning in my head, he turned to me with a knowing grin and then a nod. This, combined with the growing realization that the man *was* Charissa's maker, the shaman cannibal himself, made me shiver, cradle my arms around myself, and scooch back from him as much as I could. I surely *was* in his clutches now, and I don't think I've ever been more scared in my life. I had one little ray of hope knowing this was all to lure Chris to him, in coming after me.

The earrings tingled again; I don't know if it was in answer to the idea of Charissa in pursuit or the notion that maybe we *had* passed through some kind of portal and came out the big ocean hole. As I thought about it, I remembered that we *were* basically in the Bermuda Triangle, and maybe he, as a shaman, knew how to utilize it? Get to where he wanted to go? And if all of that held *any* water, how the hell would Chris find us now? With the pendant, somehow, was the only answer I could muster. With that, my mind went numb.

It was all too much. I was too frightened, and I really just wanted to black out again.

Figures. When I actually *wanted* to, I didn't. Since he'd already turned back around to focus on our sailing, I relaxed a little. I watched us move beyond the ocean hole and saw it receding behind us. As I did, a distant memory struck me. I thought I remembered something about a big sea hole in the middle of the Turks and Caicos Islands, which lay southeast of the Bahamas, just above Haiti. That would be more remote, and if my recall was at all accurate, some of those Cays were uninhabited and large. Wonderful. Big islands with probably more cannibals. This was just getting better by the minute.

Also as my brain was rebooting, the directional angle of Nassau to the Caicos hit me. It was a dead shot straight line of the southernmost edge of the Triangle. So the idea of portal hopping that lengthy distance by someone who might know how to harness it started to make more sense. That is, if any of this madness made any sense. And then my thoughts went blank again.

Christopher

Joe and I stood with Alyssa as she finished brokering a deal with the pilot of a sea plane she said owed her a favor. First he gave her a sizeable discount, then she paid half of the remainder for her vested interest in getting Ariyah back, and I, the other half for Charissa's return.

Ari's mother insisted she'd erred in letting Charissa go by boat and wasn't going to let us repeat that mistake now that we were here and ready to do this. Though basically having just met us, she took both of us into her for a group hug, wishing us Godspeed. I naturally replied, "And also to you."

As we got underway and were boarding, I let Joe handle the introductions and pleasantries while I reviewed the latest texts from Charissa. She indicated what she was about to attempt in accessing a portal of the Bermuda Triangle that she believed she'd seen her maker and Ariyah go through. Stunned, I frantically returned it with a message of, "Please wait, we've procured a seaplane, we'll come to you. Wherever you are, don't do it."

"No can do, my priest," she messaged back. "Mustn't lose them. If I wait for you, most certainly shall. Fly a course that will lead you from where I am to where I emerge. I will text you location when I come out and know where that is. As you fly, *stay out* of the Triangle, clear of its edge. *You* don't need to use it, only me."

That was all. If I were prone to curse, I would have. If I thought pleading against it further might help, I'd have done so. But I knew it wouldn't. I could only wait and pray that she'd make it through successfully and return message with the unknown course we would need to fly.

As our pilot, Captain Dave, was hitting our takeoff run, Joe looked at me in anticipation of what I'd learned on the phone. Still flabbergasted at what she was going to try, I simply told him the truth, with no sugarcoating.

"Joe," I said, laying a hand to his shoulder, "Charissa says she's going to attempt to use what she thinks is a Bermuda Triangle portal. One she believes Ariyah and her kidnapper just went through to get where they're going like some kind of shortcut."

"Whhaattt?" exclaimed Joe, clearly worried about Ari. "*Using* the Devil's Triangle like some kinda wormhole hopper? Is she out of her mind? And, what, Ariyah's already disappeared through one, you say?"

"Yes," I returned, "but you have to remember who she's with, a shaman who probably knows how to utilize such vortexes. And Charissa must be assuming that since she's his progeny, she should be able to do it too. And she doesn't want to lose them."

"I'm down with that last part, but c'mon, Padre, that's quite a stretch 'triangle vortex portals'? Don't tell me *you* believe in all that crap. And as far as *who* Ari's with, that don't make me feel much better. He *may* be a shaman, but he's a cannibal too. Even if they make it through a triangle disappearance, he could still eat her!"

"I don't think he will, though," I said. "She's his insurance policy that Charissa will go to him."

"Great, I feel *so* much better now," he replied sarcastically. "So what's the deal then? Do we know where we're flying to? Dave here's gonna wanna know soon."

I knew no one was going to like the answer, "No, not yet. Charissa will text me back when she comes out of the vortex, she says. For now, she recommends we fly presumably southeast, *outside* the lines of the Triangle."

CHAPTER 24

Charissa

If I'd been concerned about rousing the captain from my induced control before, I was *really* worried over it now. As we neared Darvisch's position where they'd disappeared, the retracted funnel had begun to descend again. Once we reached it, I feared my prompts over him might well shatter in the turmoil of what would come upon us.

As such, I'd prepared ahead of time double-checking on the first mate; he was still out but okay. Plus I reupped my influence over the captain with a fresh set of commands. Having all of that squared away, I stood like a captain myself upon the ship's bow, holding the pendant high in the air above my head. I felt like a gambler in Las Vegas, not truly knowing what my chances of winning were, yet having an awful lot riding on this roll of the dice. Ariyah presumably on the other side praying for my rescue and Christopher behind me needing to know where to fly to. No pressure.

We gained the position of where my targets had been, and then the funnel fully engulfed us. Water merged with wind and cloud, becoming one great maelstrom. Once inside, it was like a plane going through heavy air turbulence combined with a surfer going down the pipeline of a giant angry wave. A bumpy ride to say the very least, but surprisingly, *not* one which seemingly threatened to overtake, capsize, and crush us in wind and foam and spray. By now I'd no longer remained topside but had scurried back inside with the captain at the helm. I held onto him as he stayed the barreling course, both to help him maintain his tenacity as well as for a little human contact in the highly tense situation.

It seemed to have lasted only a few minutes all told when we were spat out in what I could only describe as a magically tranquil spot. We were within what appeared to be the space of a giant sinkhole *within* the sea itself.

"The Middle Caicos Ocean Hole!" the captain suddenly exclaimed, somehow knowing immediately where this was.

"Where precisely is that, sir?" I asked, needing to know as fast as I could to pass it on.

"Why, it's the Turks and Caicos Islands, ma'am, north of Haiti."

Ironically, that sounded about right to me. But I had to press further to be absolutely sure. "And where would that be in relation to where we've come from, the Bahamas?"

"Straight down the southeast line of the Triangle, little lady. Wait a minute," he paused, looking at me intently. "We just got sucked *through* it, didn't we? And you…you had me steer us right into it, didn't you? Why?"

The commotion of what we'd just experienced and the blunt questions were snapping him out of my hex again, as I'd predicted. Therefore, in direct answer to his question, and to reaffirm my will over him, I replied, "Because we still need to find my friend, sir. *Because* they would've also gone through the Triangle and sailed to the most uninhabited isle within this island chain. *Where,* sir, would that be?"

"Well," he began, succumbing to suggestion once more, "the biggest one would be East Caicos, next in line from Middle Caicos, where we are and the ocean hole is."

"That's where they'd go," I said.

"They?" he asked.

"Yes, *they,* my friend and her kidnapper," I answered.

"Kidnapped?" he exclaimed. "Well let's get a move on and get your girl back! That the way you wanna go then, boss lady?"

"Absolutely, Captain!" With that, I patted him on the shoulder as I returned topside to start keeping a lookout for them again. I paused momentarily first to let our boat begin to catch up with them and to text Christopher where he and Joe needed to go. The plan was beginning to come together, but I still felt terrible for all these friends getting sucked up in *my* dark web. All of them now so far removed from their lives and our city, now in the middle of the ocean, caught up in this damn-fool quest. Well, I couldn't worry about that anymore now. I needed to get back to it, find her, and put a stop to all of this.

These islands were some pretty big landmasses for out this way. As the ocean hole, as Cap had called it, receded behind us, we sped along the coast of Middle Caicos, quite a lengthy isle. It took a bit, but we finally saw East Caicos appear. That's when my sight at last reestablished Darvisch's boat into view. Of course, I couldn't be a hundred percent positive, having lost them through the triangle portal; it could've just been another sailboat.

The uncertainty made me want to try another trick, this time *not* involving the pendant. Since I was now in close enough proximity, I thought to try and focus mentally upon Ariyah. Though not as strong as the blood one with Chris, the bond formed sexually between us *had* proven to be capable of bridging us mentally before. If she were unconscious presently, it was possible, I surmised, to maybe pick up some imagery from her if she might, perhaps, be dreaming.

The connection didn't come immediately, but during the time we continued to close the gap, a few inklings came. There were trace images of she and Joe at O'Hare, her on planes, her at Alyssa's door, her at the marketplace and leaving with Darvisch. But I wasn't really interested in all that; I knew most of it. I sought her at the present, and yes, there she was *on* the boat within inlets of East Caicos. I saw her huddled in the little old sailboat, Darvisch there in front of her, navigating weaving and winding through the inner channels.

They were far ahead of us now, well beyond the initial shoreline. She wasn't dreaming anymore, I realized; I was seeing in real time what she was seeing, even if she herself wasn't truly conscious of it. I had to pay close attention to everything I saw as I was going to need to remember how this went for when *we* got in there.

Then suddenly, she *was* conscious, and our connection didn't break! I saw and felt her get tied up by the wrists, then hauled and dragged out of the boat; they'd made land! I was so shocked, overcome, and scared for her *I* broke our link in my intense emotion. For the first time in the entire course of this ordeal, I truly felt as though she could be in real danger.

Though I didn't scream aloud, I was on the inside, and my disheveled look on the outside got Cap's attention. "Is everything okay, ma'am?" he asked.

"Not at all, Captain," I replied. "Call it woman's intuition or whatever you like, but I just got a strong impression that my friend is in serious trouble now, with her kidnapper. Does this boat go any faster, sir?"

"Little bit but not much more really," he answered. "It ain't a speedboat."

There was no other choice then; it was time to go for a swim and make myself the speedboat. The distance ahead looked to be a good couple of miles, but I knew I could cover it faster than the trawler. I was at full strength from a fresh meal, and the time for this leisurely cat-and-mouse was over.

"Captain," I began, "I'm a good sprint/distance swimmer. I'm going to go after her *now*. Trust me, I'll beat the boat. But can you continue to East Caicos anyway and wait for me in its bay? Just follow the way I go because we'll probably still need you. Oh, and a seaplane will likely arrive before long with my other friends. Please let them know I've gone to the island."

He looked at me funny, like *sure you're fast/you're out of your mind,* but he didn't say anything. I gave him another good eye-gaze, compelling him not to freak over my inhuman speed, which he was about to observe. He acknowledged me with a nod as I bolted topside and dove into the sea.

I'd dressed appropriately enough to where what I had on wouldn't slow me down in the water—tank top and shorts. Good thing, as I wouldn't have been fond of going into the lion's den in just bra and panties.

Joe

Padre Chris had been out of sorts for most of our flight. He'd done a good job of trying to get me onboard with what Charissa had been texting him about the Triangle and all. Now all he had to do was believe it himself. And he'd been for sure worried about her big time. At least he was, till he finally got the confirmation text telling us she got through and where to go. Captain Dave was happier too.

Now I was the only one kinda beside myself. Dave hadda flight plan, Father Chris knew Charissa was okay, but we still nada on Ari. I didn't have to feel bad for not coming anymore; I just felt bad, period, scared outta my mind for her. Oh, and bad, too, for *me* being the one who took her to the airport in the first place.

I guess Father Chris must'a recognized my glumness, having just come off it himself. He came over to me and tried to offer me some comfort. "She'll be all right, you know," he began, patting my shoulder again. "Charissa's there now, wherever it is the shaman and Ariyah have gone. She'll get to her, believe me. Ariyah is the whole reason she's out here, why we're *all* out here. She won't stop till she gets her back."

I knew I was supposed to have felt reassured, and maybe I was a little bit. It was just that now I was more invested actually being here, doing this *with* them. Would've been different if I'd stayed behind like I'd originally meant to. But here, in the thick of it, the intensity was magnified, and I wasn't as easily persuaded. So whether Charissa got to her in time or not still gnawed at me.

Thankfully, Cap't Dave chimed in about then with the announcement of our arrival. Or at least he thought we were gettin' close. "The Turks and Caicos Islands, guys, on the horizon! I think you said *East* Caicos, right, Father?"

"That's right, Captain," Padre Chris replied. "She said it's uninhabited, so the trawler we're supposed to look for should be easy to spot, right?"

"Doesn't mean there won't be *any* other boats about," answered Dave. "The west side *is* uninhabited but not the northeast. Still, it'll probably be easy enough to find."

And it *was,* didn't hurt that the two on the boat were waving us down like crazy as we descended. 'Course neither one of them were Charissa, so that raised our eyebrows some. After we hit our water landing and were within earshot of the boat, the larger man shouted out, "are you Charissa's friends?"

"yes, where is she?" Father Chris shouted back.

The big guy on the boat, the captain I'd guess, waited for the plane to get as close as it could and power down the engine before he answered. "Took off sprintin' in the water to get to her friend quicker. Wanted to offer her the dinghy, but she didn't gimmie a chance. She hit the water so fast, then shot away like a bat outta hell!"

Pretty sure me n' the padre thought it together *lady-vamp speed. That* kinda confirmed to me that something prob'ly *was* wrong with Ari; Charissa wouldn't have jumped ship to beat the boat there unless things *had* gone south.

"Well, let's get to the damn island ourselves then!" I blurted, frustrated.

Turning to Dave, Chris said, "That would probably be in order, I imagine. Can you coast us in any closer?"

"The water's pretty clear here," he answered, "so yeah, we can go in further, sure."

The trawler's cap waved at us to hold up, suggesting that he should come aboard the plane, so he could help us better pinpoint where Charissa had gone in, once we got closer. He gave his first mate some instructions, to follow us I figured, but it turned out to be more than that.

The mate started unhooking their dinghy, then the cap swiveled back around to our pilot and asked him, "Can we tie the dinghy onto the back of the plane for you to drag with you? These boys are gonna need it when they get into those interior channels up in there. *That's* where their lady went."

Dave looked it over good, then decided it was manageable, I guess. He gave the cap't a thumbs up, which was passed on to the mate who then tied the dinghy on. The cap't hopped into it so he could steer as it was towed; and Dave fired up the propeller, getting us cruising again, staying grounded on the water as we started in.

As it turned out, Dave got us *all* the way to shore, which was cool, but when we saw what it looked like through all the coves and creeks leading in, Chris commented, "God's certainly been with us in this, providing just the right people and resources we need. I've got a good feeling about this."

I was glad for his observation because right up until he said it, I'd been totally Han Solo on it, having nuthin' but "a bad feeling about this." Chris had a good point; Charissa's ship crew *with* a dinghy, our pilot flyin' us in on air *and* sea—all of it coming together perfectly to get us where we needed to go when we ourselves hadn't been sure of where *that* even was! Maybe God was helpin' us out after all.

CHAPTER 25

Charissa

The "super swim" was invigorating but meandering through the winding, sometimes shallow, inlets on memory proved more of a challenge. When I'd run out of water, hitting land, I felt I'd gone roughly the right way, though I wasn't absolutely sure. Then I came upon "breadcrumbs" I wish I hadn't; blood trails and little bits of flesh. These told me I *had* taken the correct path because when I smelled them, I knew they were from Ariyah.

At first I started getting overwhelmed like I had before when I saw her being dragged out of the boat. I had to stop myself from going there because I had to keep my wits about me; I wouldn't do her much good if I turned into a blubbering wreck.

I examined the amount of blood and size of the skin chunks. I also took notice of the spacing, how frequently I was encountering the bits and spatter. They were well spaced out, dropped sparingly. Only often enough to keep me moving in the right direction. I didn't need them very regularly; my nose could do the rest to get me to the next one, and Darvisch knew this.

Determining these specifics in my tracking helped settle me that she wasn't likely enduring mortal injuries. Darvisch was doing minimum damage to her, just enough to keep me lured. Still, it pissed me off to no end that he *was* hurting her. I prayed that she'd perhaps been returned to an unconscious, zombielike state as he nibbled on her and spat out pieces.

I wound my way easterly through a barren valley of saline tundra bordered by mangrove marshes. I decided to take a look at the pendant, which I still had pocketed, to see if it might enhance my pursuit as it had helped in that regard already. Solid red but no pulsing or fluxing. Close then but not there yet. I put it up but back around my neck, rather than returning it to pocket.

While I was at it, I pulled my phone out of my other pocket, thankful I'd invested in a waterproof one. I texted Christopher to let him know where I was and to see what his progress might be. I told him I was trailing Ariyah, leaving out the gruesome parts so as not to alarm Joe. Chris replied to say they were going through the channels in the dinghy from the trawler and that the captain had joined them. I'm sure I'd noticed it on the boat before, and in hindsight, was glad I'd opted to swim myself, leaving it for them to make their way. It all seemed to be coming together. Hopefully I would soon find Ari in one piece.

The journey continued for yet a while more, rounding the valley as it curved, then crossing it entirely to make my way to a low bush forest on the other side of it. I started to waver in my earlier assessment that Ari wouldn't be too much the worse for wear as the trek progressed ever longer. With the trail still being marked sporadically with bits of her flesh and blood, I began to worry what kind of shape she'd be in when I found her.

My fears started to progress into a rage against Darvisch and what I would do to him if he should end up killing her. He *never* had to resort to this in the first place; I was going to go to him of my own accord. The whole point of that, the possibility of *forgiving* him, seemed like the very opposite of how I was feeling toward him now. I knew Chris would say all the *more* reason to pardon him, when the offense ran this deep. Yeah, right. Tell that to Joe if we should end up having to haul her corpse out of here.

Suddenly, thankfully, I pinpointed the scent of her *actual* presence close by while the pendant simultaneously vibrated and fluxed out of control. I found myself nearing one of many caves in a network of them. Entering, I found her trussed up much as she might have been in the dungeon of *my* own making back home. There had to be some kind of irony in that, but right now, with my friend hurt and bleeding, I had little interest in any such parallel. I just wanted to get her down, healed, off this God-forsaken island, and to hell with Darvisch and whatever madness he'd concocted in this game of bringing us all here.

Ariyah

I found myself coming to in another haze of confusion and, this time, in pain too. I hurt all over, and I felt it all the more as my arms were releasing from the tension of being held over my head by ropes. I thought I'd recalled being in the boat with the shaman and somehow Charissa seeing me there. Whether that was true or not, she *was* seeing me now, helping me down, holding me tight. I tried to hug her back as best I could, but it hurt so much I was wincing out tears and blood. Then I just sort of collapsed into her bosom.

I saw my arms stretch out before me as she rested me down to the ground of a cave. I was kind of shocked, seeing that bits of my skin had been gouged out, and I figured that the ache I felt over the rest of my body meant that animal hadn't stopped there!

"Wha-what happened to me, Charissa?" I asked weakly. "Was he *eating* me? What am I, an appetizer? Why didn't he just kill me and finish the whole damn meal?"

"*Very* much an appetizer, darling," she answered in a comforting tone, "he only nibbled enough of you to leave a blood trail for me to get here. I'll remember to thank him for that when I find him, then kill him for it!"

To that, I chuckled and puked all at once. The thought of bitten off chunks of me strewn all across a path for Charissa to find made me roll over on my side and vomit my guts out. Chris held me gently to the back of my shoulders as I regurgitated all I had in me, which wasn't much. I grabbed her cuddling hands that cradled me to my own and lightly held them. "You know," I said, "if he's finally allowed you to find me, that certainly means he's gotta be close by. He hasn't gone to all this trouble getting us here to just let us go now."

"I'm well aware," Charissa began, "but don't *you* worry about that now. Concern yourself with nothing while I try to get some healing going for you." She sniffed me then, to rouse her hunger, releasing her fangs. She bit into her own wrist to draw out some blood, then started applying it to some of my wounds. When that dried up, she chomped open her other wrist to get more for the rest of me.

I must have been starting to feel better because I reached up to her, grabbed her *firmly,* and said, "Hey, don't use *all* of yourself up. You're going to need your strength to face *him.*"

"I know," she replied, "but didn't I just tell you not to worry?"

I couldn't help *but* worry, especially when I looked out the mouth of the cave that Charissa's back was turned away from while tending to me. I saw a silhouette there, just standing still, arms crossed, as if waiting. And even though I'd been in and out of consciousness the whole trip, I *knew* that figure well enough to know it was him.

I pulled Chris's face down to mine and whispered emphatically, "He's *here,* Charissa! Outside, behind you!"

"Of course, he is, honey," she said. "I can smell him. Your scent from the blood trail wasn't the only thing that drew me here. The stench of his saliva *in* it was detectable also. And I can pick up that same odor whiffing in from out there. Stay here, rest, I've got this. Oh and, take my phone, keep in touch with Christopher and Joe," she finished, smiling to that, and slid me her cell.

I gasped in emotion to hear that they'd *both* come, were even somewhere nearby maybe. I started to say something else, but Charissa put her index finger to my mouth to silence me. She slowly drew it away, moved her head down even closer, and kissed me. As she withdrew, she wiggled my earrings and simultaneously touched the pendant, then clasped both hands around her heart. I took it to silently mean we stay connected through the talisman. She rose, winked, squeezed my hand, turned about, and strode toward the cave's entrance to at last confront her maker.

CHAPTER 26

Christopher

I'd said to Joe earlier about how God was really with us as we traversed this wholly unknown course. I still believed that, but these endless streams and meandering waterways were beginning to concern me. The captain seemed to have a handle on it, but how did we *know* we were actually making the correct turns that would get us to them? It was taking a goodly amount of time that I wasn't sure we really had.

My last communication from Charissa had been informative to a degree but hadn't indicated she'd actually *found* Ariyah yet. When and if she did, what then, of the shaman? We all knew he was leading Charissa with Ari as the lure, so it was logical to assume that he would manifest once she got close. And that scared me. I imagined it was time to put on my "big boy priest pants" and prepare for battle as though he was demonic. It didn't seem to me much of a stretch, the spirit of cannibal to demon.

Still, we carried on, more land and less water finally to be seen. The captain seemed to be perking up to this as well, so all in all, I took it as an encouraging sign. The *best* sign, an absolute godsend, was my phone in fact *ringing,* not just a text alerting, a few minutes later.

"Hello, Charissa!" I exclaimed, but the voice cut me off.

"No, Father, it's Ariyah," she returned. "I'm calling from her phone, which she left with me. She's gone, went off with the shaman. I would've tried to stop her, but I've been wounded. Please don't tell Joe. I heard he's with you, I don't want him to worry. Charissa did some healing work on me, though I'm a little slow coming around.

But I *am* backtracking right now, the way we came, to try and meet up with you all."

"Why did she leave you and go with him?" I had to ask.

"Because she wanted to get me away from him and back to you. Once we regroup, I think she wants us to go back after her."

"How will you find us?" I asked her.

"Uh, I don't think that's going to be a problem, there's a perfect way for me to make the trek back, so long as you guys are coming in the right way."

I thought I heard her gulp strangely as she mentioned "the perfect way." I let it go though because I had to reply, "God only knows if we've taken the right course in. I'm just going to trust that *He's* led us on the proper path."

"I guess I'm going to have to go with that, too, Christopher," she answered. "So listen, I'm going to follow *my* trail"—she gulped out again—"and trust that God's going to lead us all to each other."

"You sound as though you've grown some in the faith, my dear," I said.

"Father, I've spent about the last six or seven hours with a vampire cannibal, who actually munched on me! Yes, I've been praying my ass off, and *yes,* been trusting God to get Charissa to me, and He did! So next He's going to get us to one another, *right?*"

"Right!" I replied with gusto. "Godspeed, Ariyah, we'll see you soon. Keep us posted to any clear landmarks that will help us rendezvous."

"You got it, Christopher, bye for now."

Joe elbowed me then, for not letting him talk to her as I hung up. "I wanted to talk to her, man! I didn't realize it was Ari and not Charissa till you were hanging up. Why didn't you—"

"I'm sorry, Joe," I replied, "I didn't think to. She's very much on task heading back to meet us as we speak. I guess I didn't want to distract her further. You'll see her again soon enough. I apologize."

"So she's okay then? And what? It's just her coming to us? What about Charissa? What happened to her?"

"*She* went with the shaman, wanted to get Ari away from him, and thought that was the best way, I suppose."

"*Or,* because he's her maker, he compelled her to go with him, just like he did Ari from long distance across the frickin' country!"

"Or that," I answered. "Perhaps a bit of both, it's hard to say. In any case, at least Ariyah is safe now. And once we reunite with her, we'll *all* go back after Charissa together."

"Wait," the captain interjected, "it's the girl who was kidnapped who's fixin' to meet us and *not* Charissa? Who'd you say she went with again? A shaman? And what was that about being her 'maker'? What the hell's this all about anyway?"

I'd already known from our previous communications that Charissa's consignment of the boatman involved her compelling him to take this journey. It was coming clear that those prompts were starting to wear off.

"You really don't want to know, sir," I offered, "it's complicated. You are under no obligation to journey with us further than this, I assure you. In fact, you've gone above and beyond already. Thank you."

"Yer welcome, and no problem! But whether you keep yer big secrets under your hat or not, I'm in all the way. Charissa's a good gal, and I like 'er, so I ain't bailin'."

Joe fist pumped on his shoulder and said, "Thanks again, Cap't, we appreciate ya!"

Charissa

We'd strolled together for some time after we'd left Ariyah at the cave, I and my maker. When I'd first approached him there outside the entrance, I had every intention to attack, beat him senseless, and rip his throat out. But then, something strange happened. He extended his arm out toward my shoulder, which I did not defend against, turned me about, began walking with his hand to the small of my back, and we strode away side by side.

I don't know if he had a power over me because he *made* me or because my original intent in coming here to him, much due to Christopher, was to perchance, forgive him. Considering the fact that, in these most recent moments, I wanted nothing more than to destroy him, my sudden, nearly domesticated behavior was puzzling, to say the least. As we moved ever onward, I began to get the sense that there was some purpose, a grander endgame perhaps, to our destination. If this intuition had any merit whatsoever, I found myself both intrigued and afraid at the same time.

And I worried as well that we were moving to a distance too far beyond a good comfort zone for my friends to find me again. But depending on *what* we were heading into, maybe I didn't want them to reach me—a path to even greater danger for them. They'd risked too much already in this insane journey, coming all the way from the windy city.

Then at last, he began speaking to me. I knew he was talking in his native cannibal vernacular, yet somehow, I was understanding him. The only thing I could possibly surmise had to do with the Holy Spirit. How, as in its first worldly incarnation in the book of Acts, it came into the apostles and others who spoke different languages, and they all understood each other. Hence, in relation to my current transformation via feeding on Christopher, *that* Holy Spirit portion from his blood was allowing me to interpret my maker's foreign tongue.

"You want to know why I've led you through all of this, my progeny?" Darvisch asked me. "Why we are here in this way?"

I turned slowly to his face, staring him down as I answered, "Somewhat, yes. However, my greater concern is *why* you had to do all of this in leading my friend across the country to here and do what you did to her, you animal! *I* was going to come to you myself, of my own accord, making the elaborate ordeal you've put us through completely unnecessary! Were you aware of that at all, *my maker?*"

He turned away from my gaze then, seemingly understanding me; and though he set his jaw firmly in defiance to my rebuttal, I noticed it quiver, just a bit. Was he…could he actually be feeling sorrowful for what he'd done to Ari?

"I owe you no apologies," he began, still appearing firm yet vulnerable. "I simply followed the course set in motion two decades ago when I placed the talisman into the possession of that little girl in Nassau. I knew she would one day meet you, befriend you, but you *yourself* have been undetectable to me for over a century. I finally activated that which I'd set in motion all those years ago in bringing her here now. I'd no idea you'd planned on seeking me out on your own. And this is the time of *the gathering*. I needed to bring you here, by her, for this migration."

I guess that was the closest to an apology as I was going to get. But wait a minute, "Migration?" I asked. "Gathering? What's going on here? Where are you taking me?"

"To your *presentation,*" he answered, "or rather, my presentation *of* you at the gathering. We vampire-cannibals migrate to a chosen location every five hundred years to present in community the progenies we've created in that allotment of time."

"Surely you jest," I replied, "what, your version of the Olympics or something? Different location every half a millennium? That's insane." I probably should have left out my personal commentary. I didn't need to agitate him over something he was clearly very serious about.

But he just turned away again, setting that stoic jawline of his. And no sense of any regret this time at all. And what did I do? Kept walking with him like some kind of imbecile. We carried on then, back into sustained silence, approaching another solid tree line. As we started into it, I could sense that beyond the trees lay our foreboding destination.

Thinking again to the Olympics parallel, I asked, "So do we compete against each other, we 'progenies'?"

"You shall see," was his only reply as he escorted me through.

CHAPTER 27

Joe

We stood in a pocket of trees somewhere between the cave Ariyah had come from and wherever Charissa was supposedly going, the four of us. Ari and I were holding each other tight while the Padre and the Cap't gave us space and talked among themselves.

"You *came,*" she sobbed to me. "I can't believe you came for me! Thank you, Joe, thank you *so* much."

"Well," I said, "I'm the one to blame for getting you off to the airport in the first place, so I kinda hadda try to make it right." Couldn't believe how honest I was being with her, but it didn't make much sense to be anything less at this point. "I ended up taking Charissa to the airport too, so I guess that makes me a double dunce. I went to see the padre 'cause I felt so guilty about it, and he just decided then and there that we *both* go after you two right away!"

"Wait a minute," she said, backing off a little, "*you're* how I got to the airport to begin with? I don't even remember! God, that asshole has had me in a robotic daze for longer than I thought! So what, I asked you to take me or something then?"

"Yeah, said you had a family emergency back in the Bahamas or some such thing."

"Son of a bitch!" she exclaimed, now tearing away from me, getting pretty pissed.

As she did, I saw what looked like wounds, bite marks maybe, but healing up, scabbing over. I moved closer back to her to see, reaching out my hand to touch one of 'em on her arm.

Sensitive or embarrassed, she moved away from me and said, "It's okay, they're better. Charissa used her vampire blood to start the healing. I'll be all right, don't worry about me. What we gotta do right now is stop milling around here and get back to her!

"Yes, indeed," Christopher piped in, roused at the mention of Charissa. "It's likely we're in the very same boat as when we started, Joe, with Charissa once again having a formidable lead on us, wherever it is she's going with that madman now. Once more, I'm at a loss as to how we're going to close that gap."

"I've got your answer," Ari began, wiggling her earrings with her fingers. "*These,* my boys, are magically connected to my old pendant, which Chris now has. They tingle when I have an intuition that's on the right track *or* when they're anywhere close to their counterpart, the gem. As I think we all know, they originated from the shaman. *He* made them and sold 'em to us when I was a kid. The fact that he's *with* Chris right now will probably boost the 'signal' strength even more, I'm thinking."

That said, she started moving to the south from where she'd come, then east, the other most possible direction she figured they could've headed. She paced a bit each way to check it out, then returned with a thumbs-up from the easterly path.

"Tingle!" she exclaimed. "It's faint, but it *is* there. That's the way we go!"

I looked at Father Chris and saw a look of apprehension on his face. No doubt an aversion to relying on "graven images" or something like that. He drew a breath like he was about to speak an objection, but I cut him off, figuring what he was gonna say.

"Hey, Padre," I began, putting a hand to his arm as he'd often done to me lately. "I know using the magic trinkets prob'ly break the priest rules and all, but ya gotta know it's our best bet, and I *know* you wanna find her!"

He took a deep sigh, admitting I think, that I was probably right. "You read me pretty well there, Joe," he said, "I *don't* like the idea of using them, but Charissa's been utilizing the pendant quite a bit already with effectiveness." He turned to Ari and continued, "So lead on, Ariyah. You guide and I shall pray us through the journey."

Spoken in true Father Chris style! He and I had definitely gotten a vibe for each other over the course of the trip; it was going to be interesting to see what the feel was gonna be now with all four of us. Even though she'd been hurt by that jack hole, Ari was definitely stepping up and taking charge. And why not? I think she was coming back with a vengeance from being stuck in the shaman's "zombie mode" spell for so long.

And away we went!

Charissa

I never would have believed it had I not been seeing it with my own eyes. In the beautiful island twilight, I was taking in a gathering of festival-like atmosphere. Our vampire-cannibal makers were no doubt responsible for the small village that had been erected that encircled us. *We,* the many, many progenies of our sires, spanning the last five hundred years, according to Darvisch. We were in an open meadow surrounded by forest all around it. I had to admit, it was an impressive setting, even though it was not exactly my choice to be here.

As Darvisch let me go to mingle with the others, I wondered how many of my peers had experienced as elaborate dupes as I had to finally arrive here. How many other loved ones had been threatened so that they would come. So I decided to find out. I looked around to see if I might get a sense for someone, *anyone,* that I might be drawn to.

I guess what I'd been doing for a living for so long kicked in, even if I *was* looking to give it up. I saw a man who struck me as one who I'd fancy as a client. The kind of gentleman I'd like to take into my lair, truss up, and have my way with. Perhaps I was the kind of woman he was into as well, for, as he caught me eyeing him, he smiled back. It wasn't an alluring smile, just a nice one, as if reaching out to another friendly face after a long ordeal.

I wasn't in the mood for meet and greet games, so I just cut to the chase and said, "Hello, I'm Charissa, two hundred years old, originally from London and presently in Chicago."

"Aren't you *presently* upon this Isle of Caicos?" he half-joked.

All right, I thought, *I'll allow for a little levity.* "I stand corrected," I continued. "What about you, good sir, who are you and how did you come to be here?"

"First off, the name's Daniel," he said, "and as for getting here, it's been strange. It started with dreams, then daydreams, followed by prompts and hypnotized behavior, going and doing things unconsciously, which led me to this trip. I ended up meeting my maker at like, a 'last outpost' of civilization, and he took over there in getting me the rest of the way here."

"That's interesting," I replied. "I have a similar story, except that *my* maker took over my best friend with the hypnosis, leading *her* here as a lure to draw me out. And let me tell you, it's been quite an ordeal. She's still on the island, returned to my allies I've brought with after he was done with her."

"Allies?" he asked. "For what, to break you out of here? Are they vampires as well?"

"No, all mortals—the captain of the ship I consigned to come here, my priest, my friend and her boyfriend."

"Your priest? I don't follow."

"*That's* a long story for another time. The point is, I came here with help to seek out my maker and get my friend back, that's all. I knew nothing of this *gathering*."

"I don't think many of us did. I really don't get why they're doing it. To do like a census of the vampire population they've created over time or something?"

"That makes good sense, Daniel, absolutely. And perhaps, beyond that, an assessment of who among the makers are growing 'the cause,' like multilevel marketing. Which of them advance by the success of *their* progenies adding to the populace by siring more themselves. If that's anywhere *near* the mark, my maker will be sorely disappointed for all his trouble getting me here as I've fully turned very few.

"I've engaged in a long-time vocation by which I could feed but *not* turn those who sustain me, so as to live a quiet, nonmurderous lifestyle. I went on something of a rampage when I first turned, but once I got myself under control, I found it shameful and unsavory, so I became a dominatrix instead."

Once I uttered the word, Daniel looked at me strangely, letting his imagination run with that. I could see the wheels churning in his mind and then saw the light bulb go on, having fully done the math.

"Well, that's certainly a 'creative' solution," he said, wryly smiling, "but do you not find that role to be 'unsavory' as well?"

"At first it certainly was," I replied. "But over time, it struck me as less and less so. It achieved my goals, as well as offering me a lucrative income. All in all, I counted it simply as a necessary evil, such as many of the compromises people make in modern life. That is, up until recently when I've grown at odds with it once more."

"Ah," said Daniel, the wheels continuing to spin. "Your priest, I suspect?"

"Indeed, Daniel," I replied, "and the God whom he serves, as I once did myself long ago. Ever since I drank his blood and gave him some of mine to heal the bite, I've been changing."

"How's that?"

"You know how it is that *we* as 'night creatures' may only enter another's abode when invited? Well, I've come to see Christ in much the same fashion through the experience with my priest. The Lord 'asks' if He may come into us, and if we acquiesce, He does so, sharing His cleansing blood much like we would do, and 'turns' us. Do you see? I know it sounds a lot like the typical dogma, but I *am* literally transforming. I can now withstand the sunlight! I've spent most of my journey here in it!"

"That's intriguing. And you say this all came about by the comingling of your blood and the priest's. Does the padre have a name?"

"Oh yes, my apologies. He is Father Christopher."

And as soon as I spoke his name, I suddenly had a sense of him nearby. I felt Ariyah, too, my intrinsic bond with the both of them allowing me to clearly sense their close proximity.

"What is it?" asked Daniel, picking up I was onto something.

"Christopher and my other companions, they're close at hand. I can *feel* them."

"Well," Daniel replied, "they'd better stay hidden because *something* is happening. Look."

No sooner had he said so, we both saw all the makers taking positions around the perimeter of our assembly. Darvisch and a couple of others clad and marked like him seemed to take point over the entire assemblage. Of the three, one began to speak to us, while Darvisch and the other mumbled and chanted, seemingly pouring out their shaman magics, to what purpose, still as yet unknown.

I looked about across the congregation, seeing people from all places of the world, then looked back to our makers, the cannibals. I suddenly realized that the shamans were casting forth the ability for us all to understand them in their foreign tongue, much as I'd understood Darvisch earlier by way of the Holy Spirit. Though only an educated guess at best, it was spot-on, as Daniel and I clearly understood the man, as though speaking to us in English.

"Welcome, everyone," he began. "Some of you know why we're here, some may be completely bewildered, and many are likely somewhere in-between. This is *the gathering,* where we as sires bring forth our progenies from around the world in presentation to each other and to *Maybouya.*"

"Maybouya, who's that?" whispered Daniel, confused.

"Not sure," I replied, "one of their deities, I'd suspect. A fairly common theme in my life of late." I chuckled. But what the shaman said next was no laughing matter.

"For many centuries, we shamans trained and worked to protect our people from and do battle *against* Maybouya, to appease him to leave us alone, sparing us his evil. Ultimately, there came a time when the spells we used to keep him at bay were turned upon us, evolving our cannibalism into vampirism, thereby bringing about a harmony with him, versus subjugation.

"Now rather than living and working to protect our mortal tribes from Maybouya, we grow and proliferate our *undead* tribe, working in *unison* with him, no longer ever in fear of his wrath. Thus, all of you, our progenies, are here to gather in presentation to one another as a great extended family and unto him."

Wow, I thought.

CHAPTER 28

Ariyah

From our vantage point in the perimeter woods surrounding the clearing where Charissa and all the other vamps were, we could see and hear *everything.* At least I could, but I think I had the advantage of the earrings' connection to the pendant, probably "tuning" me into Chris and what she heard. Once the cannibals and shaman took over the festivities, we scratched any immediate ideas we might've had about moving in.

"You guys getting all this," I began to ask, touching Christopher's shoulder, "or is it just me, with my 'connector jewelry' to Chris's letting me in on what she's hearing down there?"

"It's just you," Joe answered, "I'm gettin' nuthin'."

The other two nodded in agreement. Christopher's head nod was different from the captain's, though. It didn't stop. It kept bobbing some more and swaying. He sort of seemed like he was slipping away from us a little. I couldn't quite put my finger on it, but then something struck me. It looked a bit like one of those religious experiences people get sometimes when they get swept away in intense worship. But from what little I know on the subject, I thought that kind of thing was more associated with those nondenominational places, *not* Catholics.

Either way, whatever it was, continued. He stood up from our crouched position in the bushes where we hid and began moving forward *toward* the clearing we were staking out! The captain was just stunned, didn't know what to do; but Joe and I tried to grab at Christopher and hold him back. But he was determined, like on some sudden mission from God or something. He quickly pulled away, leaving us grasping at air. I wanted to shout out, scream his name, maybe go after him even; but I was afraid that more than *one* of us crashing the party might heighten their alert to us, thereby endangering him even more.

Joe, having gotten pretty close with Christopher over the journey, started to bolt after him anyway, but I managed to hold *him* back at least. "Don't, honey," I said, "whatever he's doing will just get worse for him if we *all* go busting in. Remember, that's a hive of cannibals and vampires down there!"

"Exactly!" barked Joe. "On his own, he's toast!"

"Maybe he's *not* alone," I answered. "Maybe he's got God on his side plus Charissa!"

"I thought *you* were the one 'tuned' into her through the magic jewelry," he said.

"I *am,* but who knows? The *blood* bond between the two of them may be even stronger than that. Could be something's cooking between them and God above that we know nothing about."

"Well, I dunno nuthin' 'bout *any* of all this mumbo-jumbo," the captain interjected, "but I'm with the girl on this one, Joey! Hold up till we *know* what the heck's goin' on, I say."

To that, I nodded myself, then pressed my forehead into Joe's while holding his face in my hands, trying to lull him into the holding pattern we needed to take.

Christopher

I wasn't really sure *what* I was doing leaving my companions like that. But the moment Ariyah put her hand to me, I suddenly picked up what was going on before us. It must have been her connection to Charissa via the earrings to the pendant, allowing me to get an impression of what was about to take place. And that being, the shaman calling forth their false god, Maybouya.

I didn't know how or why, but I instantly felt the Holy Ghost's calling urging *me* to action to somehow intervene. I knew at last what Ariyah must've been experiencing over the past couple of days being taken over unconsciously by Darvisch's prompts to traverse this long journey. Now *I* was traversing from the safety of our hiding place to centerstage before the entire gathering.

Fear and trepidation should have been my companions as I marched singularly through the crowd of vampires, but they weren't. The Lord was my Shepherd as He herded me directly toward front and center, before *everyone*. Just prior to reaching it, I passed through the front rows, where I found Charissa staring at me, aghast. I reached out my hand to hers as I went by, and she took it, following behind me in my procession forward. I felt her uncertainty as to what was transpiring suddenly diminish as we touched and proceeded unto the shamans before us.

And *that* was the thing that allayed all the fears I should have felt in doing what I was, *the shamans*. I *understood* them, everything they'd been saying or chanting from the moment I'd set out from my friends back in the trees. Being a man of the cloth, I know this to be one of the key characteristics of the Holy Spirit—the ability to bridge the gap of language among men to hear and speak another's foreign tongue. After all, that's what he did in his original incarnation in Acts.

And now came my act, my supreme leap of faith, with my lady, the vampiress, by my side as I addressed a throng of them. I'm not sure why the shamans allowed me/us pause as we made our way before everyone, but from the moment I announced "I am *not* the god Maybouya," the respite granted us by them came to an abrupt end. One would have thought I wouldn't have gotten another word out after that with the way the shamans rushed us then; but Charissa, somehow, had my back.

So I went on and said, "I *am* Father Christopher Williams of the Lord God Jesus Christ. To those of you here today against your will, to those who didn't *ask* for this life as a creature of the night, I beseech you to reclaim your will! You do *not* have to appease your makers nor this god of theirs through your continued participation in this gathering. Do as my companion here has done and seek the Lord of Light as she has."

Charissa

"Oh, make this about me," I said snidely to Chris with my back to him, facing the shamans on all sides. They were trying to pounce like crazy on us ever since Christopher opened his mouth, no surprise. What *was* the surprise was the fact that Darvisch and the others had even allowed us to come up. I myself was shocked when my priest appeared out of nowhere, brazenly waltzing right into the thick of things. I'd already had the sense that he'd been close by, but I hadn't expected such a move as that. When he passed me and took my hand, what else could I do?

The answer was, doing what I was doing now facing off the shamans, about eight of them, all told. Too many of them to hold off hand-to-hand, so once more, I had the inkling to try out the pendant to see what else it could do. I mean, it *did* magnetize us straight into a portal funnel earlier, so I figured, why not? A good call as it was apparently working. I had them all frozen as it were, simply by holding the pendant up, like I had before in the Triangle. Not so much frozen really, as much as *very* slow motion so the effort on their part was still there to get to us. It was simply like watching paint dry.

Still the fact that they *were* gaining small inches bit by bit was a concern. This wouldn't hold them off forever, so I concentrated all the more, simultaneously praying that Christopher's plea to my assembled brethren would ultimately garner us more numbers to take a fighting stand whenever it was the pendant might fail.

He nodded to my quip and continued, "This woman has seen firsthand the fruits of the power of Christ's blood," obviously referring to his belief in the transubstantiation process, my drinking of *his* blood transmuting into the *actual* blood of Jesus. "Old habits are falling away," he went on. "Methods she has previously used to conduct her life are becoming distasteful. She's actually come here to forgive her maker, *and* she literally is able to move about *in* the daylight!"

That last one certainly got their attention. The one before got mine *here to forgive Darvisch.* It seemed to get his as well. We looked at each other oddly; he appeared to be understanding Christopher as clearly as I was. He had that vulnerable look like he did earlier walking with me. Then just like before, he set his jaw hard again, seemingly turning his attention elsewhere. It was as if he sensed something maybe. Like I did when I felt Chris close by. Oh no. The earrings. Ariyah. He could be picking up on her nearing us. Just as Chris had come, she and the others probably weren't far either. Darvisch might—

Stop. Refocus. Stay on task and concentrate. They will all break free of this stasis if my mind's wandering all over the place. Not to mention that the other nonshaman cannibals were now looking to make a move on us as well. Keep talking, Christopher, *keep talking, win them over. I've never needed them before, but I need my vampire clan now.* But apparently, Chris had little more to say. Instead, he began moving *into* the assembled group of vampires barring out his arms, offering up his wrists. "Take, drink," he said.

No! I thought. *Are you insane? They'll drain you dry!* The shock of the sacrifice he was offering, himself, took my memories all the way back to those centuries ago when *I* was emptied of my lifeblood by a group of monsters like these. And with this, my focus in what I was doing completely broke down, and a domino series of events came crashing together all at once.

First, as I began losing the hold the pendant and I had on the shamans, the inches they'd been gaining turned into feet, and they were nearly upon me. Darvisch was the first to regain full movement and took full advantage by whipping the pendant out of my grasp while simultaneously pulling Ariyah out of her hiding place with a gesture from his other arm. She was whisked off her feet and yanked in our direction as though an object in outer space on some orbital path. It was entirely surreal as the earrings flew off of her lobes and into Darvisch's waiting hand.

One would have thought that had been all she wrote for us, but in the next instant, a good-size cluster of vampires moved forth to meet the onslaught of shamans and cannibals, with my friend Daniel in the lead no less. Some had the trickle of Christopher's fresh blood on their mouths, others who had not participated in drinking from him simply in for the good fight. As with most altar calls, not everybody comes forward; much to my relief, for I don't know that Chris would have survived had they *all* drunk of him.

CHAPTER 29

Joe

And then there were two, me n' the cap't. First we lose the padre, then Ari goes flying out of our stakeout spot too. I couldn't believe it. So finally we moved out also; no point in hidin' out anymore with all the craziness goin' down, and our friends in trouble.

Outta the gate I wanted to go after Ari, but the cap't waved me off, pointing me to go see to Father Chris as he took off toward Charissa and Ari, gun in hand. I bent down to where Christopher knelt, kinda out of it from the vamps feeding on him. Crazy bastard. I took it easy as I approached 'cause there were still bloodsuckers surrounding him, but it seemed like they were done drinkin'. "You insane, man?" I asked. "What the heck were you thinkin'?"

"It's okay, Joe," he said, "I'm well, considering. I don't know how or why, but they've treated it such as the normal taking of Communion. Just sips, not guzzling me as though a meal."

The vamps around him nodded to me in agreement with that. Who were these guys, "Casper(s), the Friendly Vamps"? Or maybe this God thing was for real, and the Man really was lookin' out for us.

As was pretty regular at this point, Father grabbed my arm and said, "Go see to Ariyah and Charissa. I'm fine here for now." Again, the other vamps nodded yeah, a couple of 'em even gettin' up to come with me.

So with a "you got it, man," I took off with my vamp escorts to go see what was up with the girls. Didn't take long to find out either. Once we got around the vamp pack taking on the cannibals, we came up to a proverbial Mexican standoff with Darvisch holding Ari by the collar, the cap't aiming to shoot him, and Charissa ready to pounce on him! They were all pretty focused on each other, so they didn't notice us at first. I decided to use that, plus how pissed I was that the asshole had her *again* to shout out Ari's name and hopefully distract Darv enough for Cap or Chris to make a move. It worked and thankfully didn't get Ari hurt or killed in the process.

It was great and gruesome, and it all happened so fast it was practically a blur. Cap't fired off what seemed like a full round straight into Darv's throat, and while the penetration was still fresh, Charissa leapt at him with cheetah-like speed and snapped his neck, leaving his head dangling half off! Chris's impact into him threw Ari clear, and I ran in to scoop her up and farther away from the skirmish.

We huddled together a short distance away, her and I. Just like that cheetah I'd compared her to, Charissa hovered over Darvisch just like a big cat who'd made the killing strike on her prey. She craned her head back and let out a chilling shriek, but somehow, it didn't seem like it was out of the satisfaction of having gotten her target. It was more like regretful, irritated.

I think it kinda spooked the cap't, 'cause he started moving away from her and backed up more toward us. There was no doubt about it; she got everybody's attention with that scream. Sure, the gunfire did too but her howl pretty much stopped everyone in their tracks!

Charissa

Well, I'd really gone and done it now. It seemed I'd brought everything to a standstill in my cry of frustration. From the journey here to making land, tracking my victimized friend to finally meeting my maker, I'd been bouncing back and forth from forgiving Darvisch to killing him. Appearing to have done the latter, all that this trip was supposed to have led to now seemed like an utter waste, as he lay unmoving before me. And the anguish I felt due to that was what made me shout out so.

Seeing what I'd done, the remaining shamans scowled at me, then gathered amongst themselves and began to chant. It was eerie, and though I had no idea what they were up to, I knew that it couldn't be good. It wasn't. As I briefly became aware that both Christopher and Daniel had made their way over to our proximity, I was suddenly *fully* aware that the dead Darvisch was *not!* His body started to quiver as the shamans' mantra grew ever louder and stronger. His half-severed head started to horrifically reattach. Then his eyelids popped open, revealing even more inhuman eyes than his cannibal visage already made them. They were a fiery dark red and filled with fury at me!

In one moment, I'd heard Christopher's utterance of "Holy Mother of God!" from behind me, and in the next, I found myself being hurled in midair *to* him with a fling from Darvisch's wrist. The thing was, I didn't think it *was* Darvisch anymore. As he caught me, Christopher quickly confirmed my suspicion and emphatically pronounced, "He's possessed!" And it wasn't hard to figure out by whom. In all likelihood, it was the one the shamans had called Maybouya, their god.

Christopher slipped a little as he helped me up, still weak from blood loss, I suspected. He caught himself nonetheless, then crossed himself as though prepping to go into priestly action against the demon in Darvisch.

"Wait just a minute there, Father," I said, holding him back. "You're not ready. You just fed yourself as Communion to a slew of vampires. You'll be too weak"

"When we are weak, *He* is strong," he said, contradicting me.

"Be that as it may," I replied, "don't be foolish. *I* will replenish you first," I resolved, biting open my wrist and shoving it to his mouth. "Take, drink. We're intermingled and intertwined enough in this now that I *know* it will help. Don't argue."

He looked at me with initial hesitation and distaste, but I suppose concluded that it was pointless to debate me on this. And at last, *he* drank of *me.* As he finished, he shuddered with what I'd guessed was a jolt of energy, closing his eyes momentarily in its surge. Before he could open them again, I pressed my lips hard into his, a kiss for luck going into battle against a demon. And for me.

We came out of our clinch amidst another round of gunfire from the captain at 'Maybou-visch.' "You guys need to pay attention, not stand there smoochin' like nuthin's goin' on 'round ya," he scolded. No sooner had he said than he went flying off his feet just as I had moments ago from the wave of a hand from my possessed maker. He landed fittingly next to Ariyah and Joe.

And with that, Maybou-visch was upon us. He eyed me curiously, giving me the distinct impression that what I'd perceived before as his fury might instead be an intense intrigue in me.

"I *like* this one," he slathered, grazing his fingers across the hair above my forehead. He felt his throat also, feeling the wound from the decapitation I'd wrought upon Darvisch, and he smiled wickedly, knowingly connecting it to me. I'd understood what he'd said, so I knew the Spirit was still at work. And in reading his twisted grin, I surmised he was some kind of chaos demon. One that had little interest in those who serve and called upon him, rather, only thriving upon the utmost bedlam he can create.

"Brutally killing your own maker in a fit of rage, very good," he continued, patting his hand to my cheek. "These fools have brought me a fine offering this day!"

I grabbed his hand to pull it away, but he flipped my wrist over along with the rest of me, slamming me to the ground for my affront in touching him.

Christopher was livid. Not a good emotional place to start for casting out a demon. "Leave her alone!" he shouted, getting ready to shove into Maybou-visch. Of course, the next thing you knew, Chris was piled alongside the captain with Joe and Ari.

As Maybou-visch moved to pull me back up, I caught Daniel in my peripheral getting ready to try the same thing in my defense. I waved him off as the cannibal demon began to drag me with him back up to the front. Looking to Daniel as I was led away, I spun my fingers in a circle as a signal to him to rally up the vamp pack again. I wasn't sure what good that might do, but knew it had a better shot than him becoming another bowling pin for Maybou-visch to knock down.

So once again I found myself there at the front of the gathering, this time being presented before everyone as Maybouya's prized pet. It felt similar to me as the vision in the mirror at my brownstone—Darvisch behind me lavishing over his creation. Now some demon god doing the same thing in *his* body. Even more revolting than before.

"See this vixen in all her glory and *your* full potential, my friends," he began. "Of any who have been presented to me, she alone has shown the kind of reckless abandon I seek and crave. So progenies, *turn* on your makers. Sires, do the same unto your children if you like. Let chaos reign, let blood flow!"

And there it was, his full-blown madness, his true intent toward all of us—to create a full-fledged massacre! No loyalty to the shamans who called him forth, no appreciation to all the other makers' labors in gathering their progenies here for him. Nothing but a raw impulse to take their efforts and make mayhem and carnage out of it. And standing in between him and that were myself and my man of God.

My first move wasn't going to appear any smarter than my previous one, but within it was more strategy than anyone could've perceived. I'd seen what I wanted when he'd knocked me down before, *where* the pendant and earrings were upon his person which Darvisch had snatched away from Ari and I earlier. I'd tried to get them back when he'd hoisted me back up on my feet, but there hadn't been enough time between spotting them and making the play.

I spun around from my presentation position, my back to him, and looked at him face-to-face. He immediately caught the rebelliousness in my eyes as I rashly challenged, "Then start with me, Maybouya," I called him for short. "Bring it, demon, battle me!"

He gave me first a wicked grin, which quickly turned to a dreadful snarl as he lunged headlong into me, hurling us both in a trajectory to plow us into the advancing Christopher.

CHAPTER 30

Christopher

I couldn't say whether or not I had a specific plan as I moved toward the possessed Darvisch; I was probably operating more on my protective instincts toward Charissa. Seeing him first holding her, then grappling with her had more to do with my action than that of entering into the exorcism procedure. Regardless, *that* was what was before me and the time was *now!* Of course, it would have to wait until I regained my footing from the collision of him and her into me. I was knocked down and to the side as they continued to wrestle with each other on the ground next to me. I very nearly interjected myself immediately to get him off her, but some kind of prompt inside my head stopped me.

Wait for it, Christopher, I heard Charissa silently say within me, *not yet, almost there!* And then I made my move, slamming myself into his side, breaking the two of them up; no small task, for he was incredibly strong. I was down again from that impact but quickly turned about to see if Charissa was all right. That was when I saw what she'd been up to. She was hastily putting on the pendant *and* the earrings. It appeared that her tussle with him had been an attempt to retrieve the jewelry, which he must've taken from her and Ariyah at some point.

The observation must've clearly distracted me as the next thing I knew, I was being hoisted up and hurled away again. I landed hard near our little group once more. This was getting to be too predictable. Charissa dashed back over to me, and for the first time since we'd been on the island, our whole team was back together. Ariyah moved to hug Charissa, but Chris offered only her a quick pat before turning back to me.

"Sorry, m'love," she said, "no time, I must first speak to Christopher. Chris," she continued, "take my hand and bring forth your crucifix. We shall bring together *all* of our talismans as a powerful combination to purge this beast!"

Joe had pointed out before my aversions to use of the magiks in Darvisch's trinkets, but I was way past that now. I'd seen enough of their potency by this point, and now I actually welcomed the notion of combining them with the power of Christ! Thus, together, hand-in-hand and holding our icons, Charissa and I were ready to begin as Maybou-visch was nearly upon us once more.

"Most glorious prince of the heavenly armies, Saint Michael the Archangel," I recited, "defend us in our battle against principalities and powers, against the rulers of this world of darkness, against the spirits of wickedness in the high places. Behold the Cross of the Lord, flee bands of enemies. The Lion of the tribe of Judah, the offspring of David, hath conquered. May Thy mercy, Lord, descend upon us. As great as our hope in Thee. We drive you from us, whoever you may be, unclean spirits, all satanic powers, all infernal invaders, all wicked legions, assemblies, and sects. Christ, God's word made flesh, commands you, He who, to save our race outdone through your envy, humbled Himself, becoming obedient even unto death. He who has built His church on the firm rock and declared that the gates of hell shall not prevail against Her because He *will* dwell with Her all days even to the end of the world."

The words were having some effect but not wholly. Maybou-visch lunged at us, but Charissa met his advance with equal force as I continued on, "The sacred sign of the Cross commands you, as does also the power of the mysteries of the Christian faith. The glorious Mother of God, the Virgin Mary, commands you. She, who by her humility and from the first moment of her immaculate conception, crushed your proud head. The faith of the holy apostles Peter and Paul and of the other apostles commands you, the blood of the martyrs, and the pious intercession of all the saints command you."

Charissa was trying to wrestle Maybou-visch down to the ground where I might dominate over him as I trudged on through my recital. In his superior strength though, he halfway slipped through her grasp and began levitating. Joe, Ariyah, and the captain instinctively moved forward to try and help her, but Charissa's vampire acquaintance Daniel suddenly pushed past them, coming to her aid. She, having hold of one of the demon's legs, was joined by Daniel, taking ahold of the other. In their combined vampiric strength, they yanked him further downward as I chanted on directly before him.

"Thus, cursed dragon, and you, diabolical legions, we adjure you by the living God, by the true God, by the holy God, by the God who so loved the world that He gave up His only Son, that every soul believing in Him might not perish but have life everlasting. Stop deceiving human creatures and pouring out to them the poison of eternal damnation."

It was showing small signs of beginning to work. Maybou-visch violently thrashed around as Charissa and Daniel continued to draw him further earthbound against his levitation. But Chris had no free hand with which to hold on to nor focus upon the pendant, a key component of our plan. Seeing this, I nodded to some of the other vampire friendlies, the ones who'd taken "Communion" of me, to come up and help us in our struggle to free Charissa of her burden so she might join me in more concentrated focus.

"Begone, Satan, inventor and master of all deceit, enemy of man's salvation," Charissa chanted with me as she rejoined my side, holding out the pendant at Maybou-visch. To my surprise, she knew the words! I'd forgotten the part her past which included being a lady of the church. Still, to *know* verses of the exorcism ritual was impressive if you weren't a bona-fide priest.

I held my crucifix out strongly at him, matching Charissa's gesture. "Stoop beneath the all-powerful hand of God. Tremble and flee when we invoke the holy and terrible name of Jesus, this name which causes hell to tremble, this name to which the virtues, powers, and dominations of heaven are humbly submissive. This name which the cherubim and seraphim praise unceasingly repeating: Holy, holy, holy is the Lord, the God of Hosts."

It was happening. Our work was having a clear effect. He was finally slowly succumbing. But we weren't *there* yet. There was still a lot of fight left in him.

"God the Father commands you. God the Son commands you. God the Holy Ghost commands you," the two of us said in unison. This was normally the point in the rite when you'd really be making headway, almost at the finish line. But it was plain to me we had much farther left to go. Our last words played back in my mind: *God the Father, the Son and the Holy Ghost.* The Holy Trinity. And three icons. The cross, the pendant, and the earrings. And yet only we *two* reciting. Perhaps, just maybe, the third talisman needed to be borne by a *third* person! And who *should it be,* I thought, than the person in whose possession they'd been in for as long as I could remember, Ariyah.

I nudged Charissa and pointed toward Ari, for Chris to motion her over to us. She was confused as to my intention but quickly acquiesced regardless. A moment later, Ari stood with us. I gestured to my own ears, then pointed at Charissa's, then gestured over to Ari. Chris translated my signing perfectly, removing the earrings from herself and handing them over to the other girl, though still looking perplexed as to what my goal was.

I couldn't allow my silence to drag on for too long, lest we lose our momentum, so as I began to direct Charissa's, Ariyah's, and my own positions to encircle ourselves *around* Maybou-visch, I continued, "God of heaven, God of earth, God of angels, God of archangels, God of patriarchs, God of prophets, God of apostles, God of martyrs, God of confessors, God of virgins, God who has power to give life after death and rest after work: because there is no other God than thee and there can be no other, for Thou art the creator of all things, visible and invisible..."

Our positioning was now complete, a triad as it were, with Maybou-visch in our center while Daniel and the vampire contingent continued to hold him at bay as he still writhed and twisted in hopes of escape. Ariyah had reattached the earrings to her lobes and touched the back of her ears, pushing the rings out and forward. Charissa held out her pendant as I did also with my Cross. I went on to finish the paragraph I'd begun, "Whose reign there shall be no end, we humbly prostrate ourselves before Thy glorious majesty, and we beseech Thee to deliver us by Thy power from all the tyranny of the infernal spirits, from their snares, their lies, and their furious wickedness."

I paused then, letting down my Cross and pointed with both hands to my lady partners for them to chant the previous along with me, "God the Father commands you. God the Son commands you. God the Holy Ghost commands you." I signaled them to recite it again as I led, holding up my Cross once more. "God the Father commands you. God the Son commands you. God the Holy Ghost commands you." As would a conductor, I continued to motion them to repeat, then repeat again, until we'd achieved a cyclical, ongoing mantra. Even our vampire ground crew began chanting with us as well. I'd have thought there could've been a serious aversion for them in the repetition of God's name across their lips, that it might melt them away or something. But it didn't. If anything, their might grew, they seemed to power Maybou-visch even further down to the ground. Maybe drinking my blood and Christ through me did the trick for the night children.

And so it seemed my intuition that the invocation of the Trinity paired with the three charms had proven its merit. It was working. Maybou-visch's struggles were slowing down to crawl, though still accompanied by the occasional violent spasm, as if still trying to rally back. Thus we kept going: "God the Father commands you. God the Son commands you. God the Holy Ghost commands you."

We pressed on for probably five minutes more as Maybou-visch's struggles, grunts, and groans faded into nothingness. "God the Father commands you. God the Son commands you. God the Holy Ghost commands you." At last, like a doctor making the pronouncement of time of death, I concluded, "It is finished. Deign, O Lord, to grant us Thy powerful protection and to keep us safe and sound. We beseech Thee through Jesus Christ Our Lord."

Silence fell over the assemblage—shamans, cannibals, vampires, our own little group even. The makers and progenies not with us began to back off in retreat while we all started to allow our breaths to catch. I released my crucifix, as did Charissa with her pendant. Ariyah slowly drew her hands away from her earrings. The captain, who'd had his gun drawn all the while, lowered his weapon. The vampires with us let loose their iron grips on Maybou-visch's body, letting it relax to rest upon the ground.

As everyone began to do just that, relax, Charissa leaned down to the corpse, which now presumably was only Darvisch. She touched him hesitantly yet with purpose just the same. I ventured she was grappling with what we'd previously spoken of as the core of this entire endeavor—the forgiveness of her maker. She reached her hand gently over his forehead and across his cheek.

His hand reached up and grabbed her wrist in a blur like a vice.

CHAPTER 31

Charissa

"You fools," he spat at me, his black eyes open once again, the demon spirit clearly *not* purged as he tightened his grip upon my wrist. He began to reach for my throat, but I intercepted the move, crashing my forearm down hard on his, pinning him down. We were face-to-face. "Christopher! Ariyah!" I shouted out. "Come to me *now!*"

Maybou-visch reared his head back in maniacal laughter at me. I spun my body clockwise around and over his, kicking out my legs to the side, still keeping what was now my elbow upon his arm, the maneuver helping me dislodge my hand from his. With it free, I tore off my pendant and slammed it into his forehead, beginning to recite our familiar chant once more.

Christopher and Ariyah were already chanting along with as they returned to me. I gestured for Chris to place his cross over Maybou-visch's heart, and to Ari the earrings to his lower extremities. She must have been feeling vengeful, for she smacked them down hard over his groin.

"God the Father commands you. God the Son commands you. God the Holy Ghost commands you." To this, and our actions upon his person, his diabolical laughter had reached fever pitch. Doubtless anticipating he would quickly dispatch us. But he didn't. No question he intended to, but that was before what happened next.

Though I was resolute in our recital of that key phrase of the rite, I was not *so* concentrated that I couldn't sense him tense prior to his move to throw us all off of him. He wouldn't get the chance, however, as all the talismans began to burst forth light and energy. It started from where Christopher held the Cross over his heart. Light shot out in both directions from the top, bottom, and sides of the crucifix. The golden beam met my pendant at his head and Ari's earrings at his privates. When it did, both our pieces glowed their brilliant blue druzy color. Between the radiance from the Cross over his heart and the illumination at his head and groin, Maybou-visch was shocked to find himself utterly incapacitated. Regardless of this magical, mysterious thing, we didn't stop chanting, only increased in volume and repetition. "God the Father commands you. God the Son commands you. God the Holy Ghost commands you." Having already caught us all off guard in his sudden resurgence, we weren't about to ease up, even if we were in awe of what was happening.

As he began to gurgle and shudder to the light wave's effects, something began to happen to *me* as well. The pendant's luminosity wrapped my body entirely, then covered me in the bluish hue. With this going on, it was hard not only for me to keep reciting, but also, it was for Christopher and Ariyah, seeing what was happening to me. Chris didn't appear as shaken over it as much as we girls; he had that smug look of confidence that God was at work, I think. As such, he looked at Ari, taking her free hand, and stared at her with focused gaze, continuing to repeat the mantra so she wouldn't fall off from it. It worked.

Observing them, it helped me, too, as I renewed myself to the chant. I looked to them both and nodded. "God the Father commands you. God the Son commands you. God the Holy Ghost commands you." In the next moment, however, I started to feel light, as if I might float away. And I *did* begin to rise, be pulled up.

Suddenly, Daniel appeared next to me and took over holding the pendant to Maybou-visch's shaking head, giving me a wink as if to say, *I've got this for you.* Winking back, I relinquished myself to whatever it was that was happening to me and let myself be pulled up to my feet. Then I started to levitate just slightly above the ground but no further.

In that instant, a growing realization occurred to me. What if this cocoon of energy and light now engulfing me *was* the culmination of all the changes that had happened to me over the last weeks, from when I *first* tasted the blood of this priest who even now, stood beside me? Could I be transfiguring from vampire to something more or something less? And why now in the middle of an exorcism? Then again, why *not* now? Momentarily, it became clear. In this present state, I believe I was likely skittering between realms, the physical and spiritual. For right then, I began to see the demon god's essence start to shake out of Darvisch. The others showed no signs that they were seeing it, which gave credence to the notion of being between dimensions within this sheath of light energy. Beyond that, Maybouya saw *me,* too, more evidence that my plane of existence had indeed shifted. He was angry and got up face-to-face with me, trying, I think, to smash his way through my cocoon to get at me. I glared back at him, in no way refraining from the chant, "God the Father commands you. God the Son commands you. God the Holy Ghost commands you!" I was screaming it at him now.

The force of my cry combined with his pounding to get through my shield suddenly struck me as a struggle counteractive, somehow con*trary* to this spiritual space we now occupied. And there was power in this blue bubble I was in; I could already feel it doing something transformative to me. All at once, I ceased my shouting, dialed it back to a softer repetition and relaxed. I spread my arms out wide as if letting down my defenses, almost beckoning him to come at me and in.

I had the sensation then that Christopher might well mistake what was happening, that Maybouya was gaining an upper hand once more and endangering me, *not* that I actually knew what I was doing, if indeed I did. I reached out in my mind to Chris to calm him, that it was all right and to continue what he was doing, unfettered. He got it, I think, for he squeezed Ari's hand reassuringly all the more as Maybouya began to enter into me.

The outer crust of my shell suddenly seemed to sizzle and crackle upon his entrance as if reacting to his negative presence. His dark specter of a spirit began to show cracks in its form, the blue light filling in the growing holes all about him. His dark eyes went wide, and then they, too, became an open gap in which the blue energy filtered through. Lastly, he attempted to curse at me, but as his mouth opened, it did so only to let out a final burst of blue, dissolving him altogether! It was horrific and beautiful all at once.

As his spirit form crumbled away, it stretched across the ovular shape of my casing and, once completely outspread, was picked up by a sudden breeze and blew away. Just like that. I let my arms down, then returned them to rest at my sides. In their dropping motion, my feet followed suit and returned to the ground as well. As I touched down, I felt the residual crackle that had dissipated Maybouya prickle the surface of my skin as the bubble began to disperse. I flushed not red but blue while this occurred, letting loose a deep exhale as the cocoon all but disappeared.

I smiled to my partners, taking the few steps between us to return to them. They stared at me as I approached, their task all but forgotten, the body they crouched over barely a memory now. I, however, was acutely aware of it, Darvisch that is. I was being drawn back to him, right where I was before Maybouya had retaken him; but this time, the pull was even stronger. And he *wasn't* gone quite yet; the reentry of the demon must've reignited whatever small spark might've been left in him. I brushed the hands of my friends as I knelt down to Darvisch, giving them leave of their charge to him. I smoothed my hands outward across his chest from where Christopher's Cross lay over his heart. The three backed away; Ariyah and Christopher appearing confused at my behavior while Daniel seemed to understand the maker/progeny bond of vampirism.

But this felt like more than that. This was the clarity at last that I *wanted* to forgive him. That which I'd battled back and forth over this whole trip and even before that. Forgive him. Hate him. Give pardon. Never. But now it *was* there, the true desire to let it all go. Moreover, it was a gnawing urge like the appetite for blood. I wanted all his darkness like I wanted someone's lifeblood, wanted to suck it out, then regurgitate it and cast it away like the dust of Maybouya's spirit into the wind. *What?*

What else happened to me in that sphere of blue light anyway? I'd have to figure it out later, though; I had business with him, and he didn't have much time left. I dropped my face to his and spoke directly, "Oh my maker, *all* of this, so unnecessary. As I told you before, I'd resigned to seek you out myself, nullifying the need to draw me here by way of kidnapping Ari. But you had other intentions obviously. This god of yours, presenting me and all of us before him. And now you've seen how that turned out. He is gone, cast out by the power of the *true* God. I've much to hold against you, but I no longer wish to. I want to do as Christ would and pardon it. All of it. Not just to me and Ari but every affront to anyone, every ugly stain on your ledger. I *hunger* for it as we do for flesh and blood. But *you* have to acknowledge it first before I can. Say you *want* the God who bested yours. And know that you cannot enter His light while your darkness remains unreconciled. You've felt the power in that light as it purged Maybouya out of you, so I ask you; do you *want* it? Do you want the *true* maker?"

I had no idea if he was still understanding me, if the Spirit's translation mode was still in play. But his eyes seemed bright as they widened, as if processing what I'd said. He nodded at me and took my hand, squeezing it. I smiled, then he smiled back. I took this to mean we were on the same page, and I could see he didn't have the strength left to speak it. I'd have to take his filth immediately before he passed, and it was gone along with him. I was operating here under the auspices of being a vampire, doing whatever it was I was doing as though I were going to drink this person's blood. I had no idea what I was actually doing, simply running on the impulses coming to me and instinct. I bent down near his neck and opened my mouth. I didn't feel my fangs protrude, and my mouth didn't land on his throat. The next thing I knew, my head had tilted upward from there, and we were face-to-face. Our lips hadn't touched but hovered close the way lovers might tease just before an intimate kiss. Unprepared, I gasped, and in so doing inhaled deeply. As I did, the intake seemed to draw out a stream of what I could only describe as dark matter out of his mouth. I reared up in shock, and the stream followed, growing longer, still funneling into me. It was like being stuck in an extended inhale as though you were a vacuum, which I guess I was.

Finally, the stream reached its end, and I was at last able to exhale. As I did, I think a burp came out along with it, and if my eyes didn't deceive me, a little puff of smoke? The last wisp of what I'd taken in I imagined. But *what* had I taken exactly and why? Why had I suddenly felt such an urge so akin to the pangs of bloodlust but for it to be a want for his transgressions? What had happened to me? In so asking, I wondered what had occurred with my fangs *not* coming out then. In hopes to put it to the test, I whirled, turning to my friends.

I dashed over to Ari, startling the bejesus out of her. I got right up in her personal space, sniffing her hard along the length of her lovely neck. She stepped back a little in surprise but overall was not off put by my invasion, only confused. Having fully taken in her scent to stir my hunger, I checked for my fangs. I didn't feel them coming out. I took both hands to my mouth but found no sharp canines between my fingers. Nothing. I moved to Christopher and repeated. Once again having taken in deeply his human scent, nothing was aroused, no fangs. They appeared to be gone. So if not a vampire any longer, what had I become?

CHAPTER 32

Christopher

"*A sin eater*," I said to Charissa. "An eighteenth- and nineteenth-century practice from Scotland, England, and Wales, where unpenanced sins of the dead or dying where 'eaten' by one who agreed to take those sins upon themselves."

"What?" Charissa exclaimed, befuddled.

"Bread and wine," I continued, "where laid out upon the body for the eater to consume by ritual, thereby taking on the person's unforgiven sins. Conceptually much akin to our transubstantiation belief of the wine *becoming* Christ's blood in Communion. Though the church itself frowned on the practice—"

She cut me off there and snapped, "I *know* full well of the ritual. I was young when it was still in practice! What I'm shocked at is the idea that you think I may have become one!"

"Forgive me," I answered, "but I heard what you said to him and saw what happened just afterward. Except for the fact you *didn't* eat food off him and *literally* sucked out his darkness, I can think of nothing else it could be."

"I didn't say I disagreed with you, Christopher," she returned. "I'm just flabbergasted that these weeks of evolution since I've fed upon you have culminated in this. I-I just don't know what to do with that."

I went to her slowly, gently wrapped my arms around her and pulled her close. "I don't know either," I whispered softly, "but we'll figure it out together."

She responded, "You're damn right we'll do it together, Father, you're half responsible for this mess after all." She winked. "It would be highly unfair for me to have to figure it out alone," she chided with a grin. She pulled back to look at me squarely and went on, "Besides, *you* were going to be my ongoing blood source since I was planning on closing up shop on the dominatrix business! Since I apparently won't need blood any longer, you'll help me figure out how to plan a diet around the sins of the dying!" She laughed and playfully butted her head into my chest and settled it in there.

Ariyah then butted herself in between us as well and added, "*I* was to be the other of that regular blood source for you, too, Chris. I have no idea what you two are talking about with this sin-eating stuff, but I'm in to help you out too."

At that point, any joking aside, Charissa teared up by her friend's support and pulled her into us, making it a group hug. She pulled Ari close and kissed her forehead. "Thank you, honey, I appreciate that. That and everything you've done for me since this started, what you've endured through all of this insanity. I love you."

Charissa moved out of our trio clinch, still with both her arms around our shoulders. She looked out into the little crowd that had gathered—Joe, the captain, Daniel, and the other vampires. "That goes for *all* of you," she said. "None of you *had* to be here other than those of you who were forced, obviously. And even then, nothing demanded you fight alongside us against the makers and the cannibal god. But those of you who *did,* my thanks, my loyalty."

Turning to the captain and, *to* that agenda, asked him, "Sir, may we offer ferry to as many of these who wish to accompany us in our departure from this isle?"

He was taken aback by the sudden shift from where all of our attention had just been, but once his brain was processing her request, he replied, "Sure, Charissa, I'll take as many as we can fit on the boat. Which *won't* be our complete capacity 'cause with ya'll being vamps, I can only use what space we've got *below* deck on account of the sun, sorry. I assume they can't all take the light like you can, hon."

"Right," answered Charissa, "thanks for thinking ahead on that, Captain."

"I was wonderin' before how *you* could be in the sun," the captain replied, "but I guess we got the answer on that just now."

"Perhaps," Chris answered, "but along with it comes just as many new questions."

"Indeed, Charissa," I said. "We should get going now though, while it's still dark, so all the night children joining us can make it back to the boat before sunrise."

"Solid plan," Joe replied to me. "Let's jam, people!" he said to everyone. Next, he held out his hand to Ariyah, and she broke away from us and joined him.

The vampires who chose to go along then joined all of us as we began to trek out of the little village the makers had made. Having seen their god purged away, they were long gone. In a few hours journey, we were, too, bidding a fond farewell to the island of East Caicos.

*****

By the time we reached the mainland, Joe, Ariyah, Charissa, and myself had traveled by way of air in Captain Dave's plane, allowing more room for all the vampires below deck of the captain's trawler. We would've liked to travel with the captain since we'd grown so close with him during the whole adventure, but it was only right to allow those who needed it to use the boat.

We waited upon our arrival in Miami for the trawler to return so as to have our final farewells with the captain, Daniel, and the vampire friends we'd made. It was early evening of the next day by then, having given the four of us some much-needed time to unwind. We'd spent time man-to-man, Joe and I; woman-to-woman Charissa and Ariyah; and as couples in our respective pairings. For our part, Charissa and I had much to discuss in regards to the end result of her final stage of transformation. We exchanged thoughts and ideas, and by the time the boat at last came back to port, we'd formulated an initial plan for when we got back to Chicago.

CHAPTER 33

Charissa

A few days later finally saw our return to our beloved windy city and our respective sectors of Old Town and Woodlawn. What had begun in these places and concluded on East Caicos had now entirely changed our lives, Christopher and I anyway. Ari and Joe would always remember the events. Who wouldn't? But my priest and I were now *utterly* altered by them. His mission and calling were diverted now at an angle directly in line to me. He had gone back to the parish to give his resignation and tie up things there. He would seek out a faith community *not* stringent on their ministers' celibacy—one that would be accepting to him taking a wife if he so chose.

At my apartment in Old Town, I spent time tearing down my dungeon and all its numerous toys and devices. I wasn't entirely certain about it yet, but I busied myself with sketches of the room as more of a spa/massage therapy studio, whether I ultimately remained here or not. I liked the vibe and could see a clearer vision of it coming together nicely. I prayed it would go so well for Christopher in his transition. Only when he was ready would I opt for us to travel back to Woodlawn and Jackson Park to do that which we'd spoken of in Miami.

He called me the next day to say he was wrapped up with his business at the church. I suggested then that we get in touch with Ariyah and Joe for them to join us at the park, perhaps today. He said that he'd already phoned Joe and that he and Ari would be available whenever we wanted to go. How about that? My priest really *was* onboard with everything we'd set forth to do. I'd joked with him on the island that it was his *responsibility* to me to have my back, but the fact that he truly *desired* to see me through these strange changes meant the world to me.

*****

We'd all met up atop the moon bridge at Jackson Park, and of course, Ariyah and Joe were curious as to what all this was about. Having already been with me during my experience in her bathtub, plus accompanying me here as well, Ari had an inkling but hadn't yet connected all the dots. Joe was entirely clueless.

We all strolled through the Garden of the Phoenix hand-in-hand, Ari and I at center holding hands and our men with their palms in ours on either side of us. Across the two of us, we caught the occasional glance of Joe to Christopher with a look of *what's up, Padre?* Finally, Christopher replied softly, "You'll see."

At last, we came to the lagoon. I broke off my clasped hand from Ari's, and Christopher and I strode off ahead of the other two. We walked headlong into the water, Christopher crouching down into it to bless it while I removed my jacket, revealing only my light jogging attire. I moved into Christopher's welcoming arms as he positioned himself as one prepared to baptize another, myself.

"What's happening?" asked Joe as he and Ari approached the water's edge. "Is he baptizing her or something?"

"Or something," Ari answered, still a little puzzled, but the light starting to dawn on her. "But I think it might be a little more than that, actually."

It was.

What Christopher and I had talked about in Miami were the ramifications of being a sin eater. That being, the load of *carrying* another's sins within them. Just as I'd been overcome in the Easter incident of Chris serving Communion and feeling as though I were taking on all the wine/blood everyone was partaking, there was the concern that carrying another's darkness would have a similar effect. My solution that Sunday was taking in holy water into myself to purge. We agreed that trying it again here, as I'd seen in my vision then, could be in order.

So here we were.

Christopher dunked me under the water, then didn't bring me back up, didn't hold me down. Just let me remain submerged of my own accord. Since I didn't appear any longer to be undead, I had no idea if what I was about to do would achieve the desired effect or kill me. I shut my eyes and inhaled. It was fire in the torrent of a deluge into my lungs, and it wasn't like before. If I stayed under and kept this up, I *would* most surely die.

But then, unexpectedly, as it happened the first time, the blue druzy sheen came over me somehow protecting me from the drowning effect that humans get when they breathe H2O into their pulmonary system. So instead of shooting out of the water suddenly choking to death, I rose from below gradually, much the same way I'd been let go from the baptismal position I'd assumed when we started. I remained rising horizontally, not planting my feet under me and coming up vertically of my own accord. And, once more, I stopped perhaps a foot above the water's surface, levitating.

"What *the hell* is happening?" exclaimed Joe to Ariyah as he pulled her tight. "This is like what happened to her on the island. Why'd they come out here to repeat it?"

"Don't think hell's got much to do with it," Ari replied. "Probably the opposite. I think she's doing that purging thing she did in my bathtub last week. She talked about maybe having to do it again *here* at some point, probably taking into herself what she took out of Darvisch necessitated that."

"Huh?" said Joe, still bewildered, never having known the *real* story of what had happened in Ari's apartment that day.

"Never mind, honey," she returned, "I'll explain later. Let's not miss whatever happens next"

And what *did* happen next *was* the opposite like Ari had said. The *opposite* of what I'd done taking *in* Darvisch's sins—now I was releasing them in like manner, a dark matter-like funnel pouring from out of my mouth up into the air. It took a little while for it all to come out, forming a decent-sized dark cloud above us. Then as our city is called, the windy, a sudden strong gust came and blew it away.

And suddenly, in an epiphany, I understood. The wind was a "toilet" flushing away the "excrement." My having "eaten" it first before, out of Darvisch, was my food. Now, unlike a blood diet, I would cycle through a meal as a human would and have a disposal of it later. This was one of those consequences Christopher and I had discussed prior to our Chicago return. That of the sad endings to sin eaters when they were around in my time. They tended to become dark, reclusive individuals, and poor wretches by the time they died.

We were determined, that if this is what I'd become supernaturally, that we take steps to prevent such an end from happening to me. Then I'd thought back to the vision I'd had purging in Ari's tub being in the Garden of the Phoenix, and it all made sense! *I'd* become as a phoenix, a sin eater out of being a vampire! One who'd taken blood, *the* substance shed for the remission of sins now taking the sins *themselves;* and having once survived on the former, the "cleansing agent" could now take the literal sin and pass it back into the heavens to the one who redeemed them in the first place.

This is what I'd concluded the earlier vision to mean, which I could not have known then. That is why we'd come back to do this *here.* We were also careful to consider what I'd attempted to do in the bathtub—*bless* the water making it holy water. And since it was we two engaging this ritual anyway, *in* a body of water, why not add the baptism element into the symbolism of my phoenix transformation? That was our conclusion at least.

And so here we were.

Since it appeared to be over, Christopher laid his hands under my body as the levitation diminished, and I dropped into his waiting arms.

A hush fell over our audience of two as Christopher carried me forth from the lagoon, as though carrying his wife over the threshold. All right, perhaps that was a stretch of my imagination, but with the way we were looking at each other as we approached our friends, it couldn't help but cross my mind.

As he sat me down to my feet, he planted a tender, caring kiss upon my lips, to which Ariyah blushed and squeezed Joe's hand tight.

He turned to her in response and started kissing her forehead down to her cheek, then moving around toward her mouth.

She playfully slapped him away chiding, "Copycat! Be original!"

We all laughed, then I moved to my friend, took her hand once more, and began to walk on out of the park. The boys resumed their handholds to us, just as we were when we came in. We left Jackson Park fulfilled, giddy, but with one of us still confused, asking, "So *what really* happened back there anyway, guys?" said Joe.

CHAPTER 34

Christopher

It was roughly six months later, and Charissa and I found ourselves running, as we're often apt to do, along Lakeshore Drive but a long way from the stretch we're used to in Old Town. We were gone from there now, though Charissa imagined she would still pursue her massage therapy notion somewhere. This particular run was a little different; we were jogging to get a break from all the grueling tasks of wedding planning among other things.

We are both traditional people, despite what Chris *used* to do for a living. We knew we wanted to be together and knew beyond a shadow of a doubt that God had brought about our union through such stark clarity that it was undeniable, and in a way that we also knew it trumped the priesthood. Despite what Frank had earlier thought, I would never find a position in a Catholic church where I could marry *after* I'd become a priest; it was only allowed if you'd already been joined *before* accepting the calling, and even then, it was rare. Thus, I found a position pastoring at the Apostolic Church of God in Woodlawn, ironically.

Being there, Chris could stay with Ariyah and I with Joe until we actually tied the knot. The four of us set out on this day together, Joe driving the I-90 Express into Chinatown and dropping us off along the South Branch Chicago River at Roosevelt. Ariyah and Joe flipped back east on Roosevelt, proceeding to Soldier Field where they attended a Bears game, while Charissa and I took the river taxi to its end where it met the Outer Drive Bridge at Lakeshore, where we then ran.

We might've already been wed by now and living apart from our friends, were the nuptials the only thing on our plate. There was, of course, the matter of my vampire-turned-sin-eater, no small thing. Charissa's "need to feed" did not frequent itself in the same fashion as did the bloodlust, however. Christians generally have an aversion to serpents due to the devil becoming one in Eden, but I would liken her eating cycle of sins to that of a snake. It was somewhere around every month to month and a half; we came to learn. The rest of the time, she consumed normal food perfectly well. She *was* fully human again, after all.

As such, I began to utilize my newfound post at the Apostolic Church as a means to facilitate what Charissa needed to do. Ergo, since there was a clearer line between being saved as opposed to being an approved Catholic, I enthusiastically volunteered for the outreach ministry to the sick and the dying. Though the vast majority of church members had received salvation, there were always the many friends and family who had not. People fall into terminal illnesses or are critically injured all the time. When we would receive prayer and visitation requests for those who were in dire straits, especially the ones who *were not* saved, we would seek them out vehemently. And in these cases, Charissa would do what she now did.

It was unorthodox to say the least, but we managed to find a way to make it work. The ritual itself was always kept secret when we performed it; as in this day and age, it was a practice that was all but extinct and would likely be viewed by most as some strange kind of voodoo. It would usually take a bit of a push, but these were people who tended to be desperate; so generally, in the end, they would be willing to give it a try. I would share my experience as a Catholic father and my greater knowledge of ritual, both old and new. I would go on to include Charissa's background as a lady of the church, not saying *when* that was, of course. My attempt was always to instill in them a confidence as to our strength *as partners,* Charissa and I, and that we were fully capable in what we were doing. Whether that was *absolutely* true or not remained to be seen as we were still on a learning curve in all of this.

This was no more apparent than today, on this run. As we rewound back to the Outer Bridge along Lakeshore where we'd looped the trail, Charissa slowed her pace down to a crawl. At first, I was concerned that she was beginning to feel the pangs of her hunger or that she was too cold. During these periods, her stamina would decline, and she'd get ill like she used to in the sun, if she'd gone too long without sustenance. It *was* growing close to time, we both knew, but this was different today.

"What is it?" I asked. "Is it getting to be that time again?"

"Close, but no, I don't think so," Charissa began, bending over, holding her knees. "This doesn't feel the same. Don't think me crazy, but I have this foreboding sense that, I don't know, someone nearby, someone *not* sick but healthy *wants* to die."

"Excuse me?" I asked, watching her in bewilderment.

She returned my gaze, looking at me equally puzzled.

"Some kind of sixth sense or something, you think?" I offered.

"Yes, perhaps," she answered. "I'm sorry, I don't know what to do exactly."

"If I may suggest," I began, trying my best to think on my feet, "why don't you take a couple of steps in a few different directions from here and see what you get. Ariyah did something similar back on the island with her earrings, trying to use them as a locator to your pendant. It's worth a try."

"Great idea!" She made the attempt, then pointed west and said, "Let's go. It's stronger this way."

So we proceeded from the Lakeshore Trail down to the River Esplanade, jogging back the way we'd come on the river taxi. She picked up her pace again, obviously reacting to whatever her sense was, as it increased. We passed the Riverview Condominiums, then the River Esplanade Park. As we cleared the Cityfront Place Apartments adjacent, we saw it—a figure leaping from maybe the twentieth story of the Sheraton Grand Chicago Building! It appeared to be a man plummeting toward certain death in the water below.

It was hard to believe Charissa wasn't a vampire anymore as she pulled away from me at what seemed like superhuman speed. As soon as she was close enough, she leapt into the water, splashing into it only moments after the man had come crashing down like a ton of bricks. I imagined this must've been what it looked like when she'd jumped into the ocean from the trawler, speeding toward East Caicos in pursuit of Ari and Darvisch.

Charissa

I hadn't expected to be *in* the river on this little excursion today; but there I was, gathering the dead weight of this poor fellow in my arms and hauling him up from below the water. As we broke the surface, to my utter shock, I saw that it was my former client, Johnathon O'Connor. Abruptly, my past and my present came flooding at me all at once. Aware that my feeding time was shortly to come anyway, combined with the sudden sense that a death by suicide was close at hand, I had come to this action of retrieving John from his probably fatal fall. Regardless, I had to try to revive my friend if I could, try to find out what could possibly have led him to a decision such as this.

Still, realizing this might likely end in a sin-eating meal, I needed to find somewhere nearby without a lot of people around, to which a good-sized crowd of witnesses had already gathered along the Esplanade, not the least of whom was Christopher. Looking about, I eyeballed the other side of the river, the Chicago Riverwalk and the underbelly of the Columbus Drive Bridge. I caught Chris's sight and pointed to him where I was going, then swam as fast as I could to the other side with my burden in tow. Upon getting out of the river and up under the bridge, I started CPR, and something stranger yet began to occur. In my hand-to-chest contact with him, *images* flowed through my mind: Of him in session with me, he and other female liaisons, an angry wife, and back on the wagon. As I switched to mouth-to-mouth, more visions came—a plummeting business, serious gambling to try and leverage it, and so on. I felt his sorrow, helplessness, depression, and regret—his unresolved *sins.*

As I moved back up to resume compressions, I saw the dark vapor trail out of his mouth and into mine, then disappear inside me. I suddenly had that full feeling letting out an unexpected burp, with that little residual puff of smoke. Shockingly, ironically, as *I did,* so did he, *coughing* up and spitting out water! We stared at each other, amazed—he that it was me of all people crouched over him, and I, that someone I'd just taken sins from *yet lived!* To this point, all my experience as this sin-eater creature was all about last rites as it were.

It was he who spoke first, "Charissa *what?* How are you—why are *you here?* Did you save me?"

I could barely get the words out; I was so beside myself at what had just happened. Finally, I managed, "*I did* in more ways than you know. I-I've been saved myself recently, I guess you could say. I was nearby with my priest turned minister who will soon be my husband. I saw someone jump out of the Sheraton Grand building into the river. When I jumped in to try and reach out it turned out to be you!"

"My dark angel," he replied, "now my angel of light, it seems."

I thought about the compliment for a second, then answered, "*Light,* eh John? Tell me, do you feel *lighter* now, in any way? As if a burden has been lifted, perhaps?"

He puzzled for a second, paused a moment more, then returned, "Why, yes, I think so—funny you should ask. Right now, seeing you, knowing what I just tried to do, I can't imagine *why* I would've thought that could be any kind of solution!"

"Good answer," I said, helping him up, and together we turned about from under the bridge toward the approaching Christopher. "That'd be the reply I was looking for, John. My work here is done." Then inexplicably, I embellished out of nowhere, "Go and sin no more."

My priest overheard that last part, nodding to me with a smile as he advanced to embrace me.

EPILOGUE

Ariyah

Football season was over; the Bears had won a playoff spot on that day we saw them while the Chrises had their own little adventure, and spring had come again. It was *their* wedding day in the Garden of the Phoenix. Christopher relished in the return to warmth and being outdoors. It seemed like the right place to me, too, having come here often enough with Charissa for her purging and even before that, of course.

Chris looked beautiful in her stunning white gown, both modern and classic all rolled up into one—*so* her. Her long dark hair seemed just a tad lighter these days; I chalk it up to her transformation. Christopher, too, looked dashing in his tux, though somehow appeared as priestly as ever to me. Joe and I were best man and maid of honor respectively, naturally.

As we stood near the bank of the lagoon and the minister was speaking his piece, Joe and I readied ourselves to present what would've been the rings, if the happy couple hadn't already chosen something different. From his shirt pocket, Joe produced *the earrings* and placed one each into Charissa's and Christopher's waiting open hands. As they both recited "With this ring, I thee wed," each of them took the single earring they held and placed upon the other's ear.

Then from around my neck, I removed *the pendant necklace* and handed it to Christopher. Next, the pastor took the Cross necklace from off his collar, handing it to Charissa. In completion of the ceremony and the unique symbolism they'd chosen for each other, Christopher put the pendant chain around Charissa's neck and she did likewise with the cross necklace around Christopher's—the talisman trio of the triune God that beat the cannibal god and pushed Charissa's transfiguration to its conclusion. It couldn't have seemed a more fitting commencement of their union if you tried.

Joe

Through everything that had happened from Chicago to the islands, the aftermath, and now this "afterglow," I hadn't really understood half of what had been going on around me with Charissa, Christopher, and Ariyah. But here today, I *got* it, at last. Over the past few months, each of them had explained to me the parts I'd missed, which made the parts I *did* know finally click. It helps when you know the whole thing.

So after the wedding, when Christopher took over to serve Communion to everyone there, it made perfect sense. Instead of a champagne toast, it was the wine and the bread. Heck, it was how it all had started between the two of them, I'd learned. And even though all the guests didn't have a clue what it all meant, the four of us *did.* It was Charissa's story in a nutshell, going from what she'd been to what she was now.

"Take, drink," said Christopher. "Take, eat."

Want more by A.F. Roberts? There is more to come! Look for **Cross-Gate** coming soon. The story of a gifted girl and her father who learn to take their peculiar dreams of the iconic symbol *as a portal* and *manifest* it into waking reality. It becomes their vehicle to cross over to the other side, via the *dream-walk* and the guidance of *the Shepherd.*

Curious as to Charissa's mysterious references to the wolf and witch from her past? See her early life as a vampire in America when she meets Emily and Erica, the aforementioned witch/wolf cousins in ***EmErica,*** on the future horizon.

Learn more at www.afroberts.com

ACKNOWLEDGEMENTS

I would like to thank the folks at Christian Faith Publishing who've been instrumental in bringing *Blood Light* to fruition. From my literary agent, publication specialist, editors, designers, to graphic artists, much thanks to all in effecting Charissa's and Christopher's story, when I never dared dream it might happen like this.

Many thanks to Pastor Ted Elsenheimer, who's progressive, congregational-participation services way back when, allowed my contribution of serving the Lord's Supper to spark the idea for this story. One Sunday while doing so, I found myself in a reflective moment as the notion of a strange metaphor between Communion and vampirism occurred. The elements, representational of *blood* and *flesh* (and *ingesting* them), got me thinking of what a vampire does to sustain their *undead existence*. And we, as humans, who are *dead in our sins*, doing the ritual to draw upon the power of Christ's *blood*, in the 'maintenance' of our *eternal* lives.

At the time, I'd never intended to make a novel of it, but after completing of the aforementioned *Cross Gate* series, I found myself needing something new to work on, thus, *Blood Light* was born. During the course of working on the project, so many more parallels struck me that I knew God had put me on the right track with this tale. A shout-out also, to all the others I served with in those services whom I remain friends with to this day. Thanks for your continued support.

As always, I thank my son Perry (an inspiration himself to the protagonist in *Cross Gate*), for his steadfast encouragement and enthusiasm to my writing.

ABOUT THE AUTHOR

A. F. Roberts was raised in Phoenix, Arizona, by transplants from Chicago. As a youth, comic books and science fiction were major influences. High school through college brought an introduction to Christianity, which, combined with the former, birthed not only a refreshment of spirit but also an imagination enhanced by stories of the Bible and theological prophecy.

Roberts studied advertising arts at Maricopa Tech/Gateway Community College, earning an AAS degree leading to positions in the field of community newspapers. His experience in both press operations and prepress layout production work occasionally resulted in photojournalism or newswriting assignments. In life, divorce and single parenting steered into journaling. In tandem, these elements began the progression into creative writing.

One day while serving communion, an idea about a possible parallel between the Lord's Supper and vampire lore occurred to Roberts. In time, the notion turned into the novel *Blood Light*. Roberts's graphics abilities have helped in website design for book promotion, potential book cover layouts, and the like.

Roberts continues to reside in Phoenix, reading and writing books and staying close to his son. He attends Living Streams Church and maintains employment in the print industry at Short Run Printing LLC, which produces magazines, books, and comics.

Lightning Source UK Ltd.
Milton Keynes UK
UKHW011903280620
365713UK00001B/93